DreamWorks

PENGUINS
OF MADAGASCAR

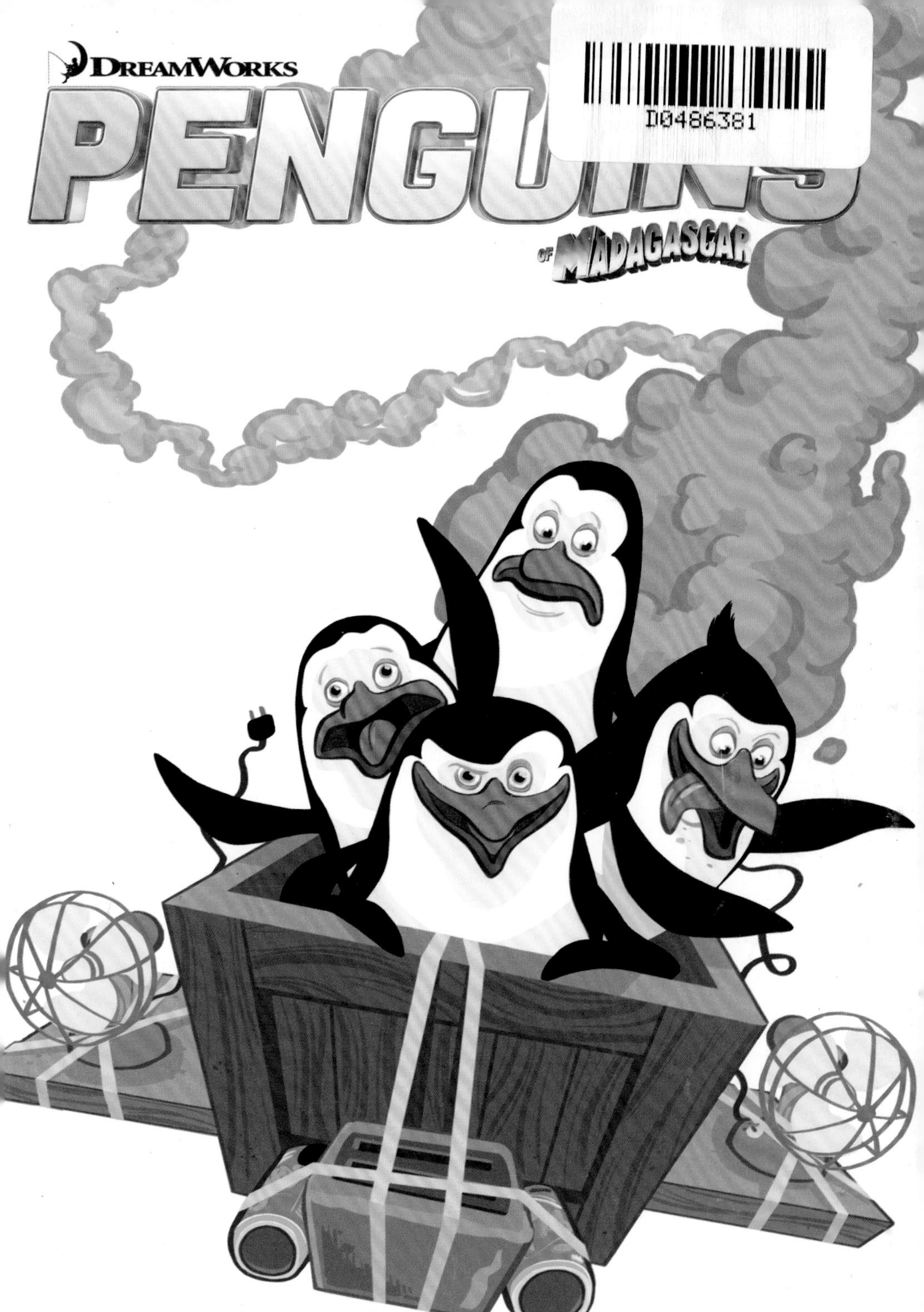

PENGUINS IN PERIL!

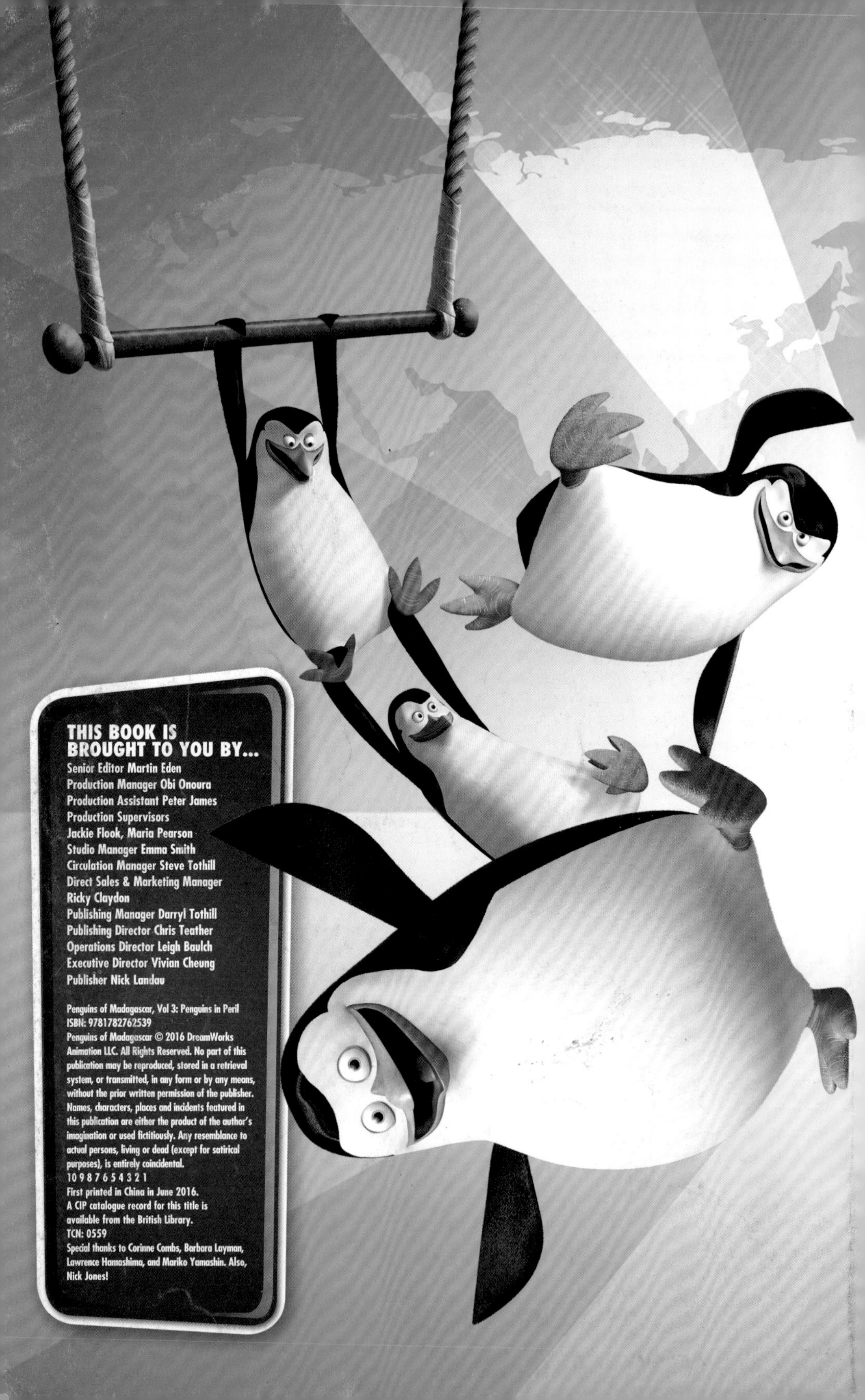

THIS BOOK IS BROUGHT TO YOU BY…

Senior Editor Martin Eden
Production Manager Obi Onoura
Production Assistant Peter James
Production Supervisors
Jackie Flook, Maria Pearson
Studio Manager Emma Smith
Circulation Manager Steve Tothill
Direct Sales & Marketing Manager
Ricky Claydon
Publishing Manager Darryl Tothill
Publishing Director Chris Teather
Operations Director Leigh Baulch
Executive Director Vivian Cheung
Publisher Nick Landau

Penguins of Madagascar, Vol 3: Penguins in Peril
ISBN: 9781782762539

10 9 8 7 6 5 4 3 2 1
First printed in China in June 2016.
A CIP catalogue record for this title is available from the British Library.
TCN: 0559
Special thanks to Corinne Combs, Barbara Layman, Lawrence Hamashima, and Mariko Yamashin. Also, Nick Jones!

DreamWorks

PENGUINS OF MADAGASCAR

Inside

2 EPIC COMIC STRIPS

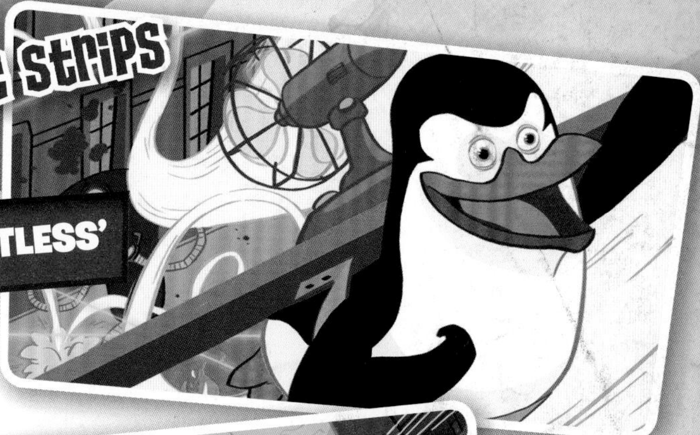

'FLIGHTLESS'

Writer:
Cavan Scott
Art and colors:
Lucas Ferreyra
Letters:
Jim Campbell

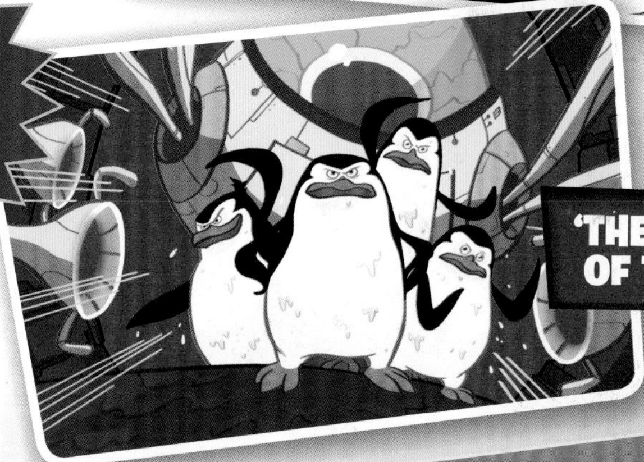

'THE ELITE-EST OF THE ELITE'

Plus

PENGUIN PRESENTS

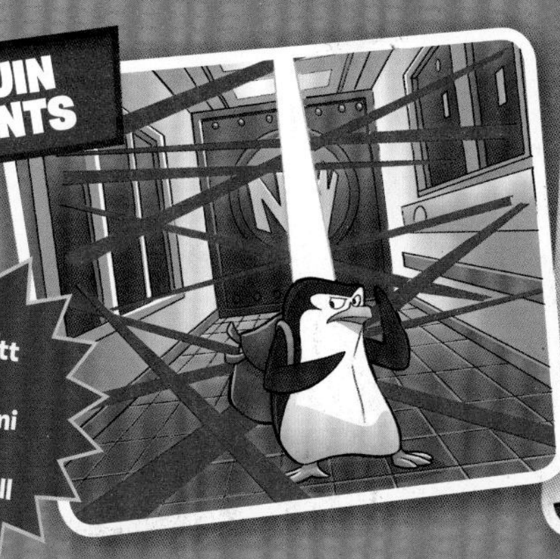

Writer:
Cavan Scott
Art:
Egle Bartolini
Letters:
Jim Campbell

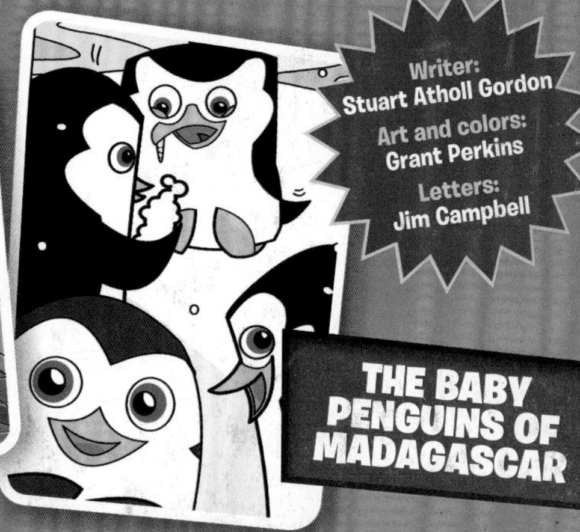

Writer:
Stuart Atholl Gordon
Art and colors:
Grant Perkins
Letters:
Jim Campbell

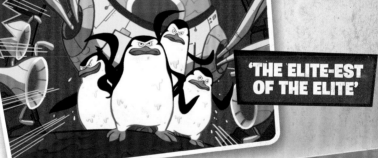

THE BABY PENGUINS OF MADAGASCAR

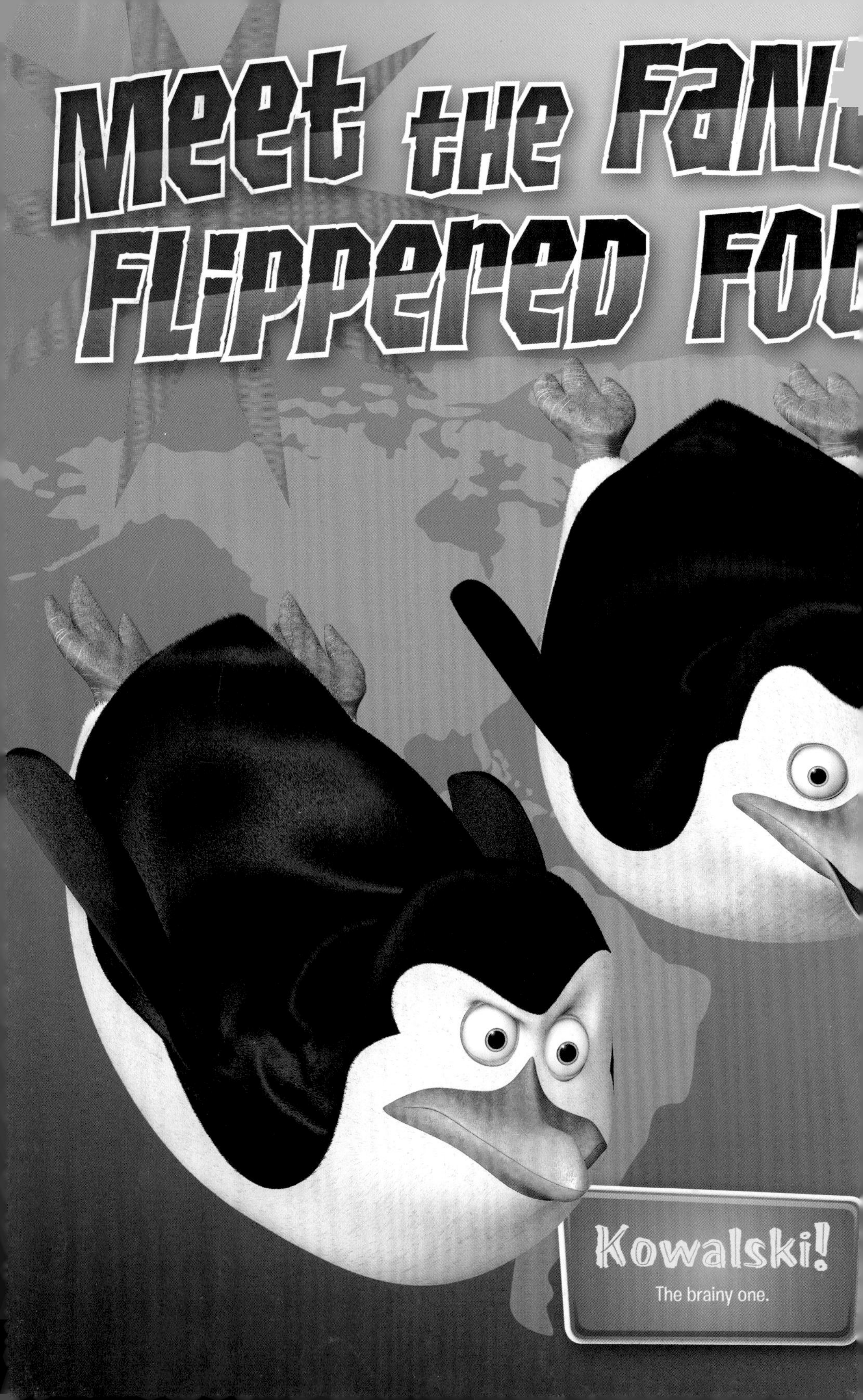
Meet the FAN
FLIPPERED FO
Kowalski!
The brainy one.

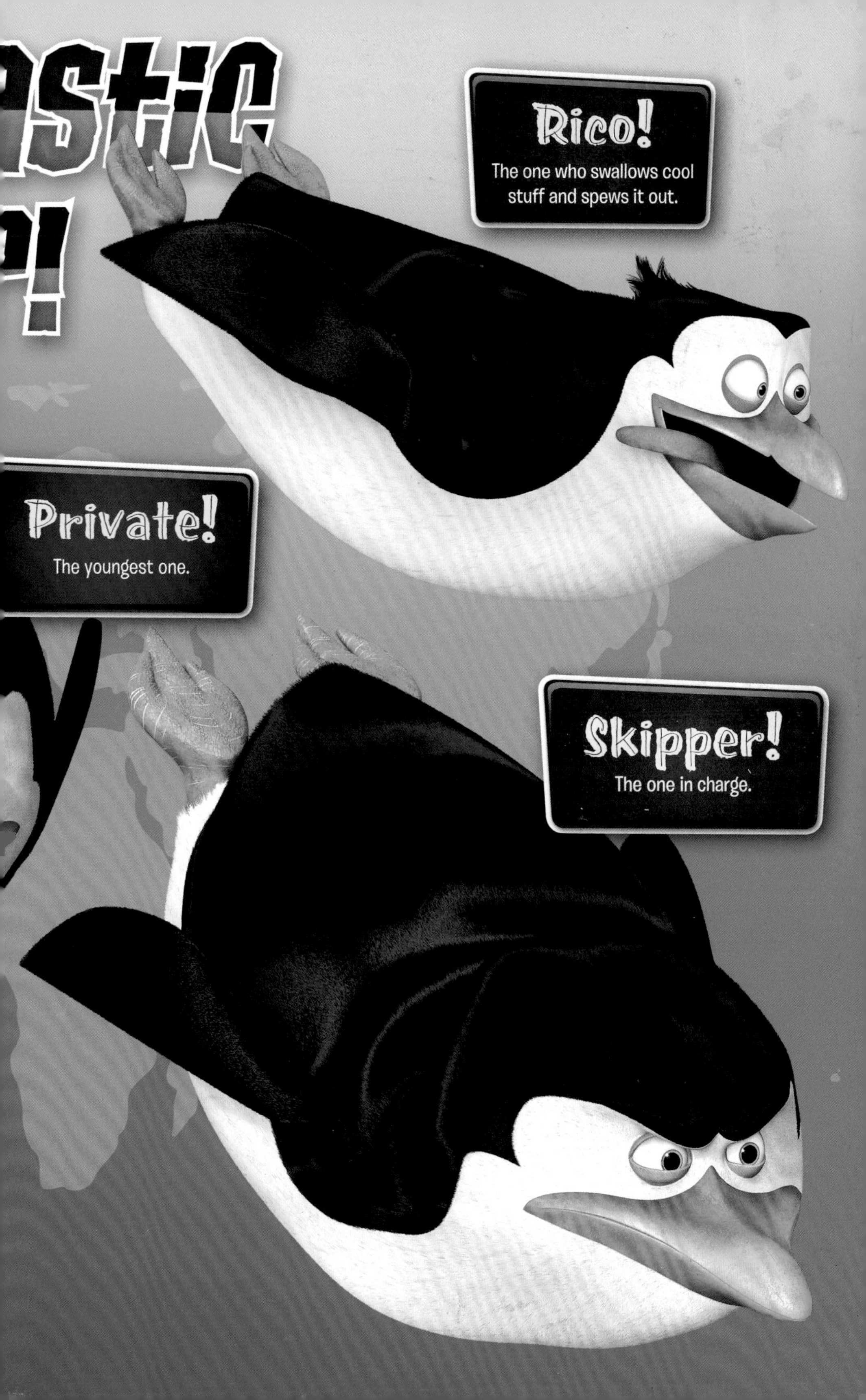
Rico!
The one who swallows cool stuff and spews it out.
Private!
The youngest one.
Skipper!
The one in charge.

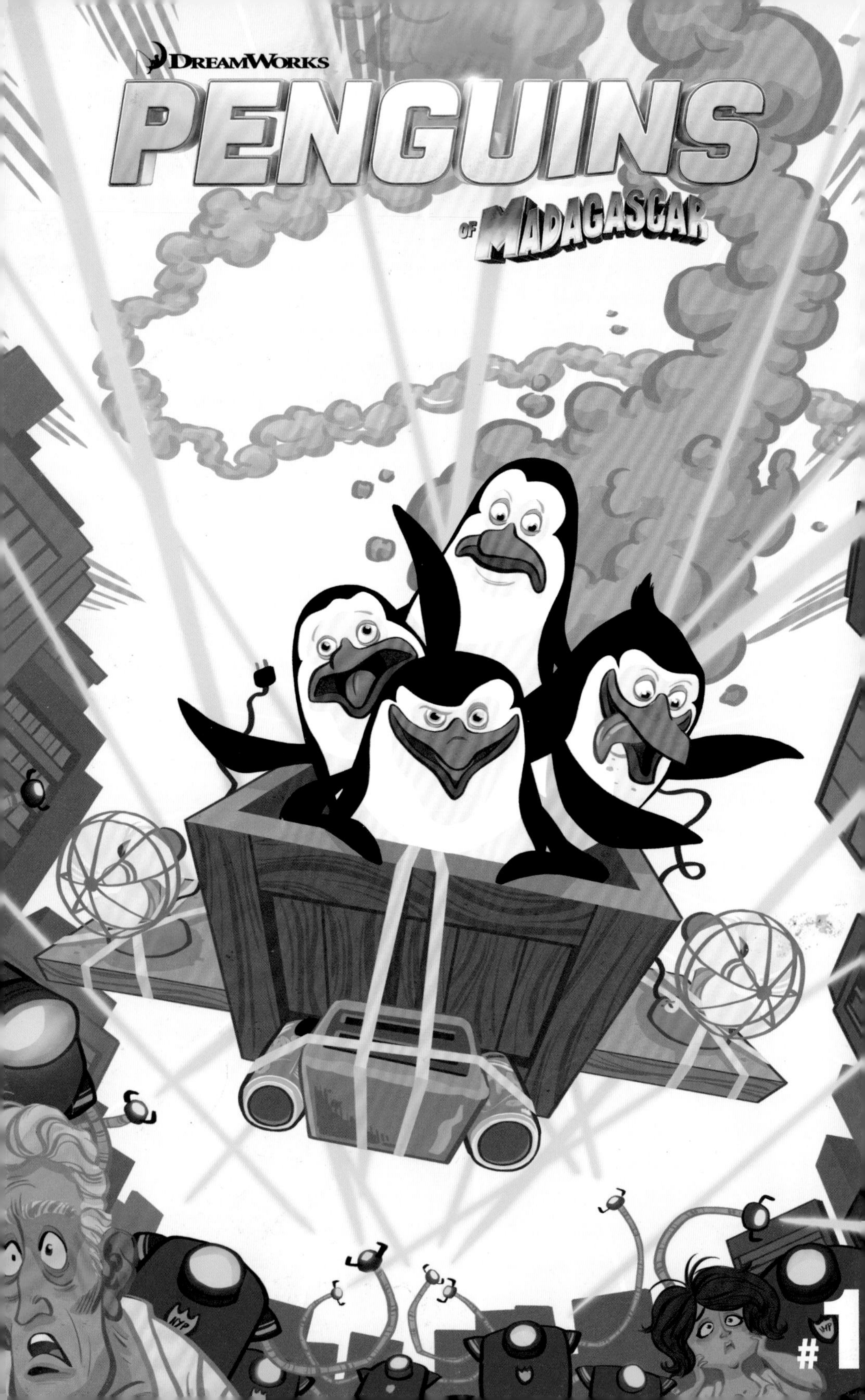
DreamWorks
PENGUINS
of MADAGASCAR
#1

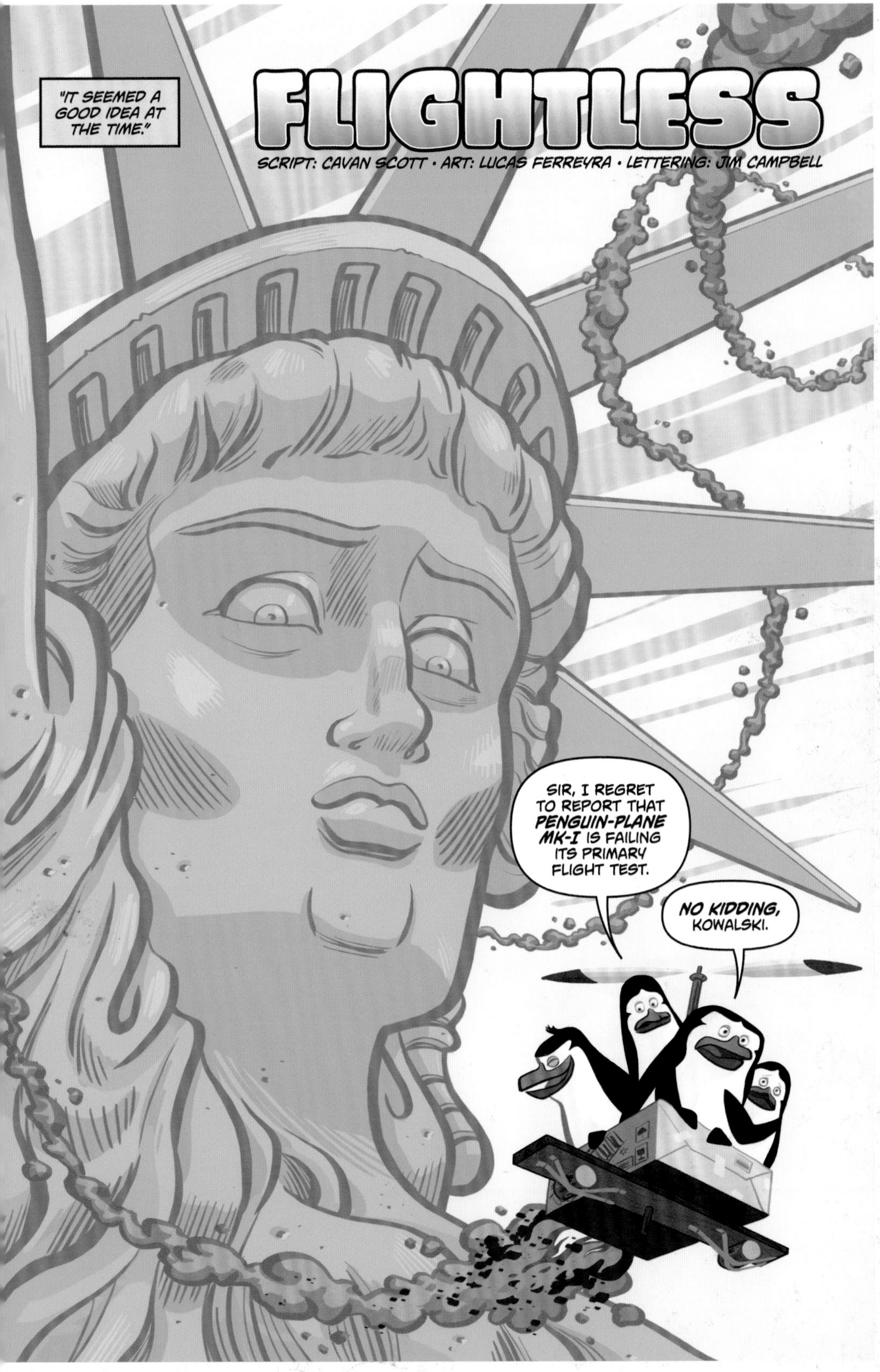
"IT SEEMED A GOOD IDEA AT THE TIME."
FLIGHTLESS
SCRIPT: CAVAN SCOTT • ART: LUCAS FERREYRA • LETTERING: JIM CAMPBELL
SIR, I REGRET TO REPORT THAT PENGUIN-PLANE MK-I IS FAILING ITS PRIMARY FLIGHT TEST.
NO KIDDING, KOWALSKI.

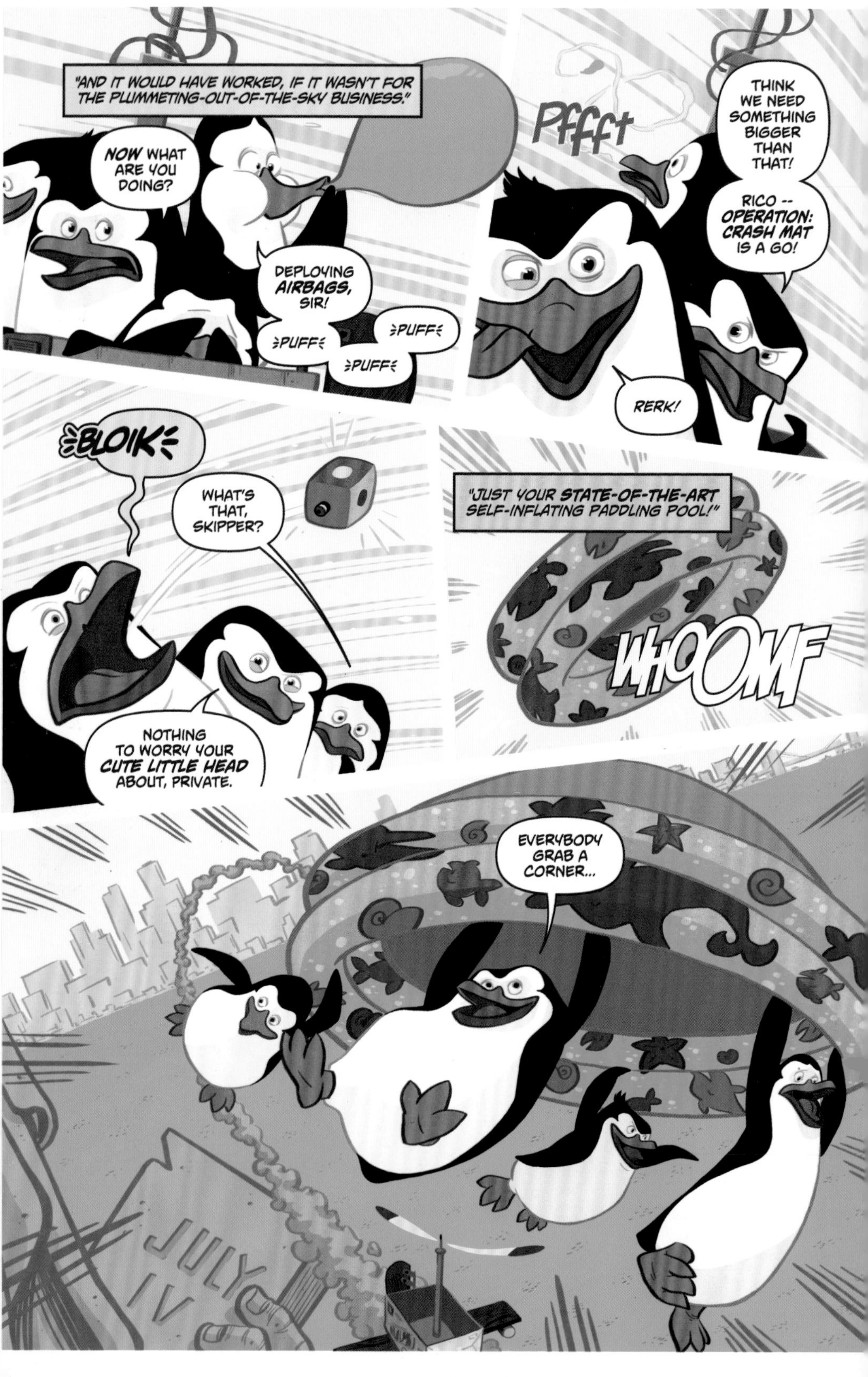
"AND IT WOULD HAVE WORKED, IF IT WASN'T FOR THE PLUMMETING-OUT-OF-THE-SKY BUSINESS."
NOW WHAT ARE YOU DOING?
DEPLOYING AIRBAGS, SIR!
PUFF
PUFF
PUFF
Pffft
THINK WE NEED SOMETHING BIGGER THAN THAT!
RICO -- OPERATION: CRASH MAT IS A GO!
RERK!
BLOIK
WHAT'S THAT, SKIPPER?
NOTHING TO WORRY YOUR CUTE LITTLE HEAD ABOUT, PRIVATE.
"JUST YOUR STATE-OF-THE-ART SELF-INFLATING PADDLING POOL!"
WHOOMF
EVERYBODY GRAB A CORNER...
JULY IV

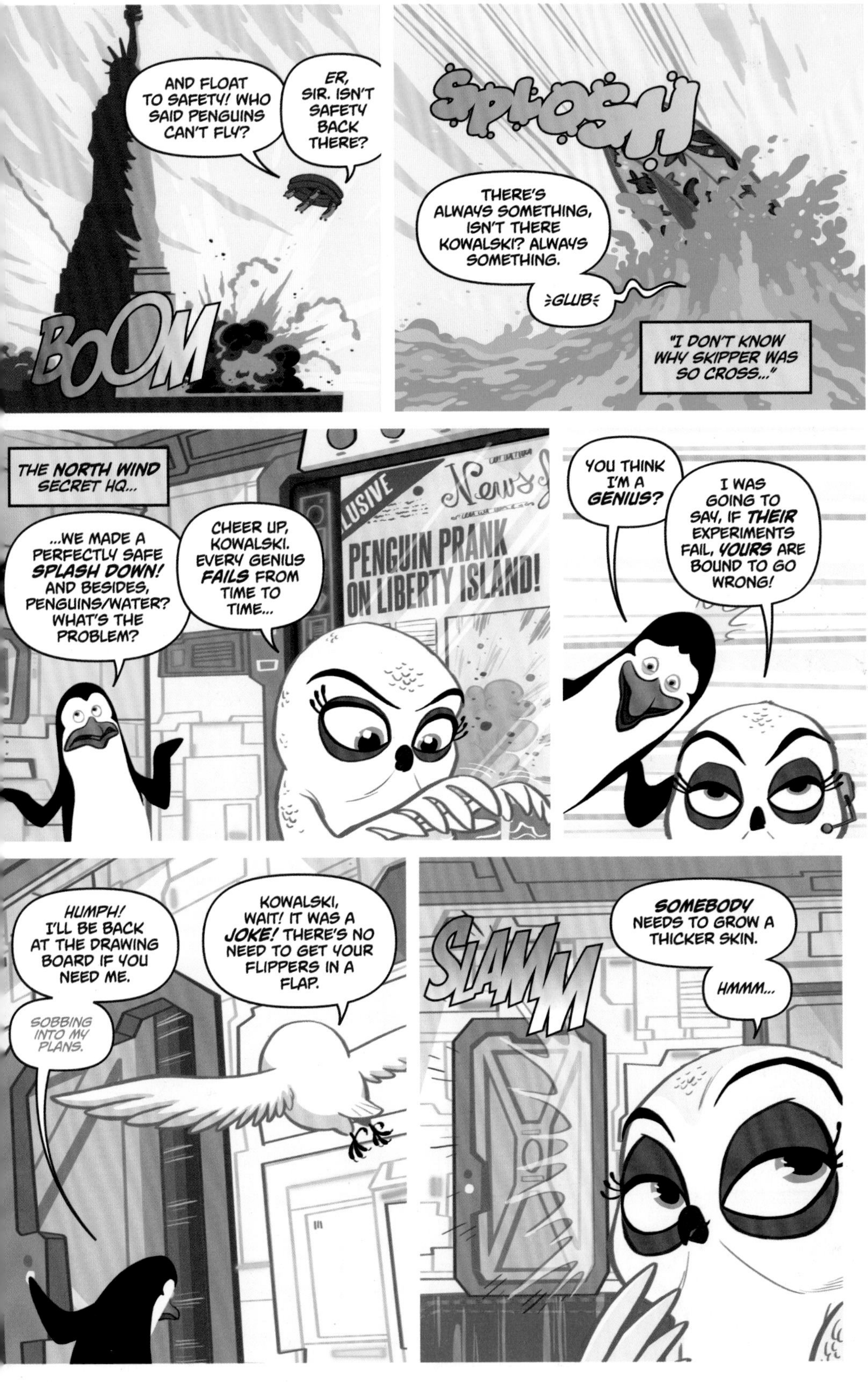
AND FLOAT TO SAFETY! WHO SAID PENGUINS CAN'T FLY?
ER, SIR. ISN'T SAFETY BACK THERE?
BOOM
SPLOSH
THERE'S ALWAYS SOMETHING, ISN'T THERE KOWALSKI? ALWAYS SOMETHING.
GLUB
"I DON'T KNOW WHY SKIPPER WAS SO CROSS..."
THE NORTH WIND SECRET HQ...
...WE MADE A PERFECTLY SAFE SPLASH DOWN! AND BESIDES, PENGUINS/WATER? WHAT'S THE PROBLEM?
CHEER UP, KOWALSKI. EVERY GENIUS FAILS FROM TIME TO TIME...
PENGUIN PRANK ON LIBERTY ISLAND!
YOU THINK I'M A GENIUS?
I WAS GOING TO SAY, IF THEIR EXPERIMENTS FAIL, YOURS ARE BOUND TO GO WRONG!
HUMPH! I'LL BE BACK AT THE DRAWING BOARD IF YOU NEED ME.
SOBBING INTO MY PLANS.
KOWALSKI, WAIT! IT WAS A JOKE! THERE'S NO NEED TO GET YOUR FLIPPERS IN A FLAP.
SLAMM
SOMEBODY NEEDS TO GROW A THICKER SKIN.
HMMM...

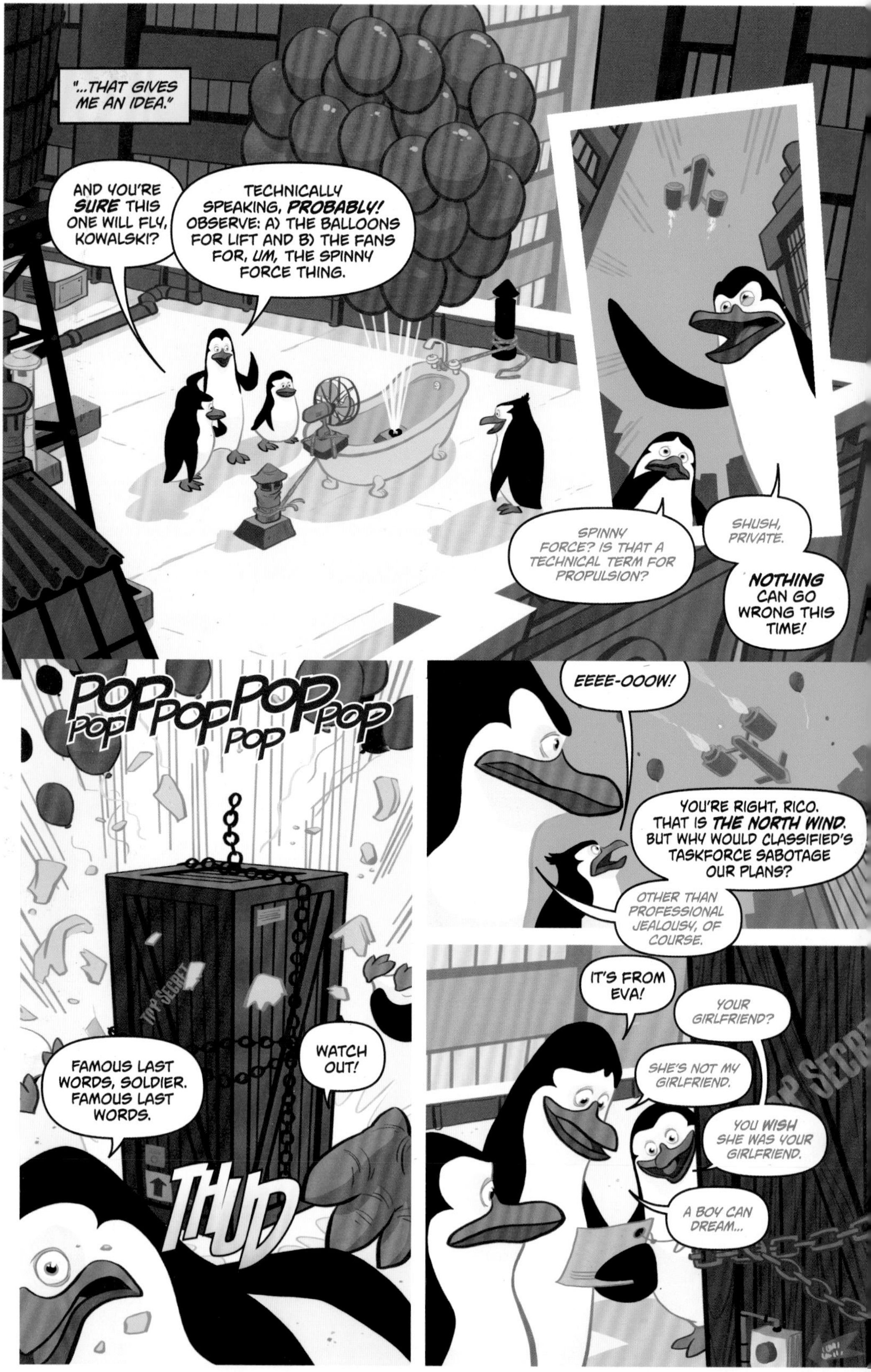
"...THAT GIVES ME AN IDEA."
AND YOU'RE **SURE** THIS ONE WILL FLY, KOWALSKI?
TECHNICALLY SPEAKING, **PROBABLY!** OBSERVE: A) THE BALLOONS FOR LIFT AND B) THE FANS FOR, *UM,* THE SPINNY FORCE THING.
SPINNY FORCE? IS THAT A TECHNICAL TERM FOR PROPULSION?
SHUSH, PRIVATE.
NOTHING CAN GO WRONG THIS TIME!
POP POP POP POP POP POP POP POP
FAMOUS LAST WORDS, SOLDIER. FAMOUS LAST WORDS.
WATCH OUT!
THUD
EEEE-OOOW!
YOU'RE RIGHT, RICO. THAT IS **THE NORTH WIND**. BUT WHY WOULD CLASSIFIED'S TASKFORCE SABOTAGE OUR PLANS?
OTHER THAN PROFESSIONAL JEALOUSY, OF COURSE.
IT'S FROM EVA!
YOUR GIRLFRIEND?
SHE'S NOT MY GIRLFRIEND.
YOU **WISH** SHE WAS YOUR GIRLFRIEND.
A BOY CAN DREAM...

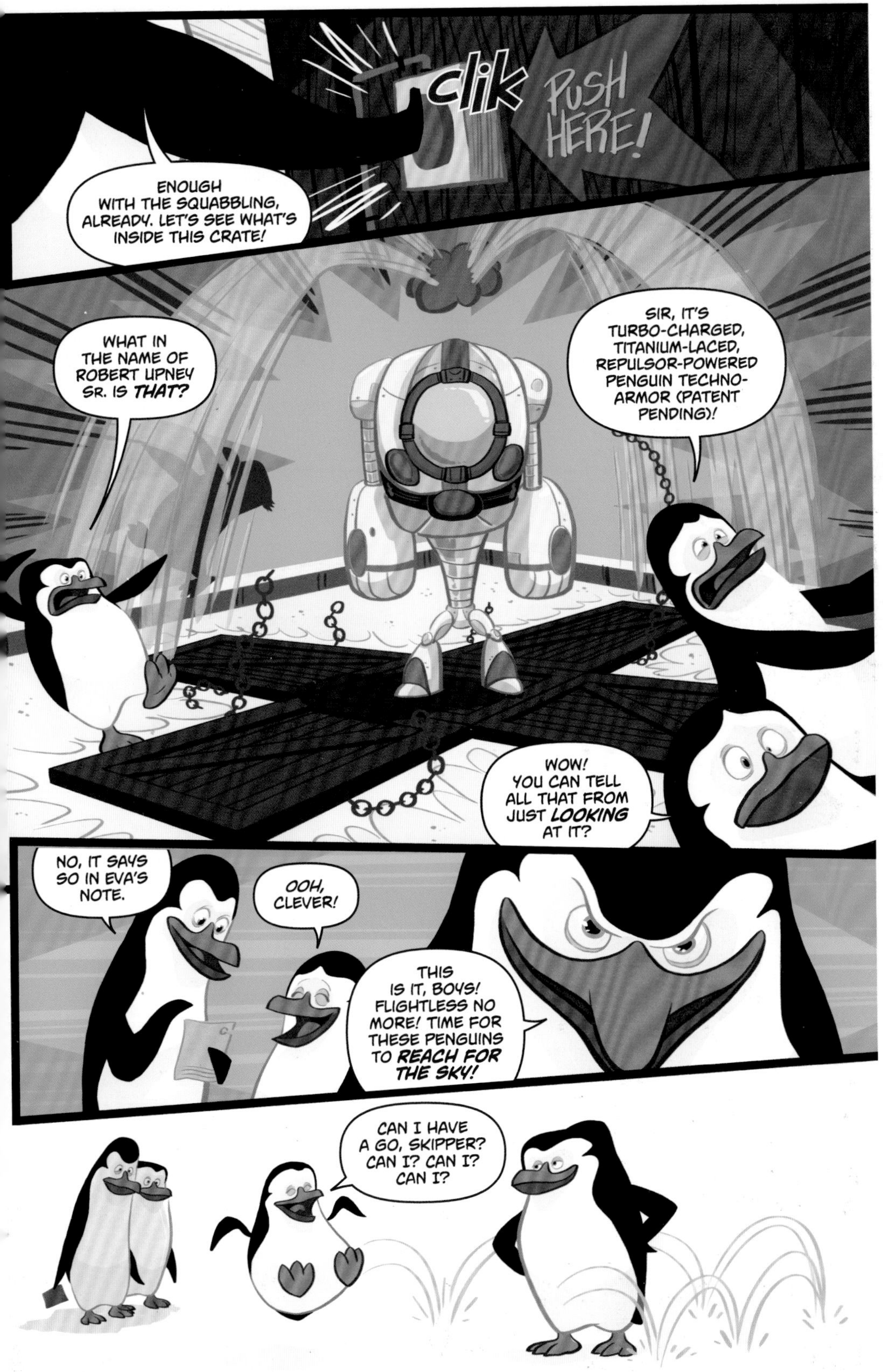
clik
PUSH HERE!
ENOUGH WITH THE SQUABBLING, ALREADY. LET'S SEE WHAT'S INSIDE THIS CRATE!
WHAT IN THE NAME OF ROBERT UPNEY SR. IS *THAT?*
SIR, IT'S TURBO-CHARGED, TITANIUM-LACED, REPULSOR-POWERED PENGUIN TECHNO-ARMOR (PATENT PENDING)!
WOW! YOU CAN TELL ALL THAT FROM JUST *LOOKING* AT IT?
NO, IT SAYS SO IN EVA'S NOTE.
OOH, CLEVER!
THIS IS IT, BOYS! FLIGHTLESS NO MORE! TIME FOR THESE PENGUINS TO ***REACH FOR THE SKY!***
CAN I HAVE A GO, SKIPPER? CAN I? CAN I? CAN I?

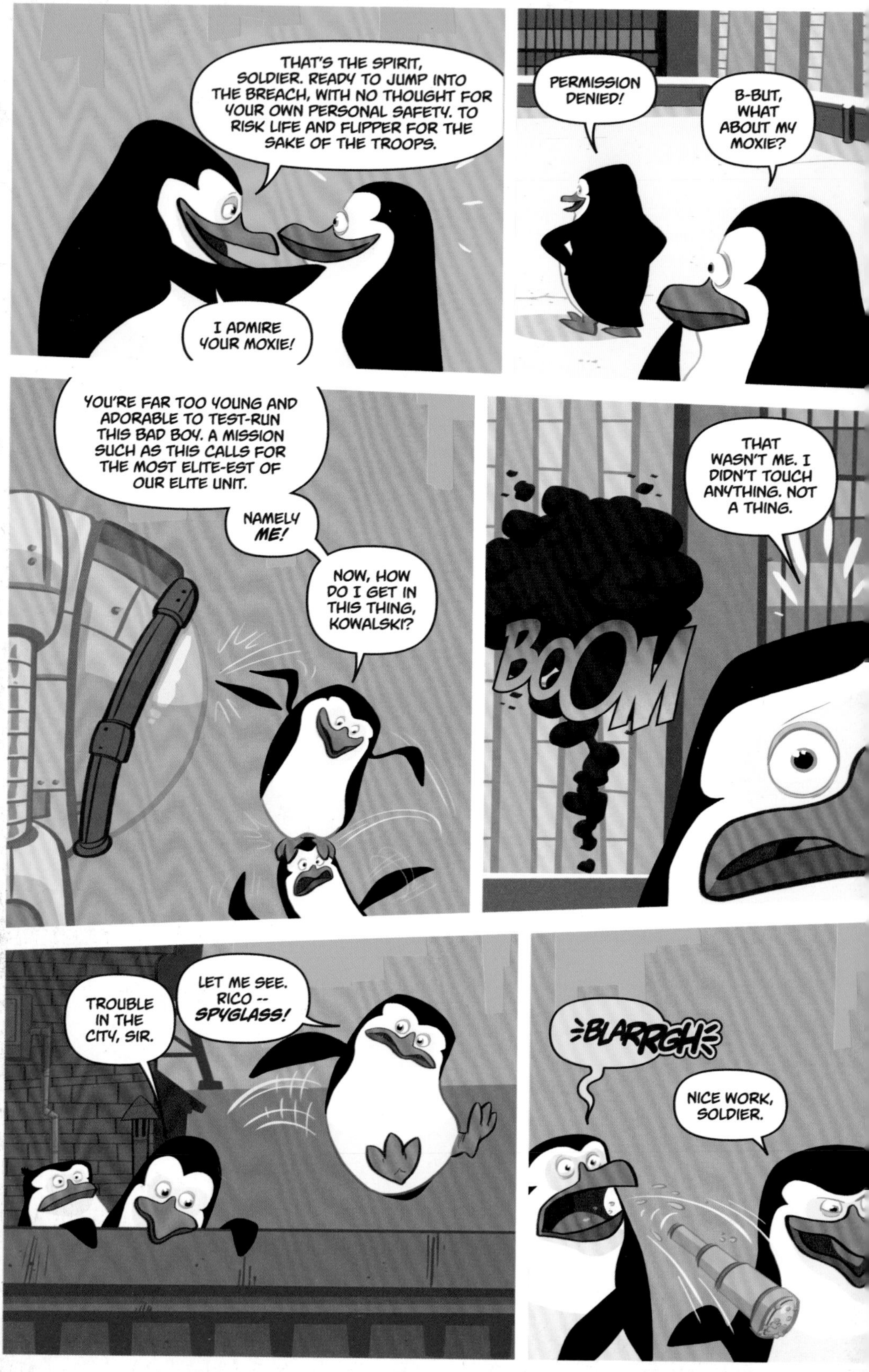
THAT'S THE SPIRIT, SOLDIER. READY TO JUMP INTO THE BREACH, WITH NO THOUGHT FOR YOUR OWN PERSONAL SAFETY. TO RISK LIFE AND FLIPPER FOR THE SAKE OF THE TROOPS.
I ADMIRE YOUR MOXIE!
PERMISSION DENIED!
B-BUT, WHAT ABOUT MY MOXIE?
YOU'RE FAR TOO YOUNG AND ADORABLE TO TEST-RUN THIS BAD BOY. A MISSION SUCH AS THIS CALLS FOR THE MOST ELITE-EST OF OUR ELITE UNIT.
NAMELY *ME!*
NOW, HOW DO I GET IN THIS THING, KOWALSKI?
BOOM
THAT WASN'T ME. I DIDN'T TOUCH ANYTHING. NOT A THING.
TROUBLE IN THE CITY, SIR.
LET ME SEE. RICO -- *SPYGLASS!*
BLARRGH
NICE WORK, SOLDIER.

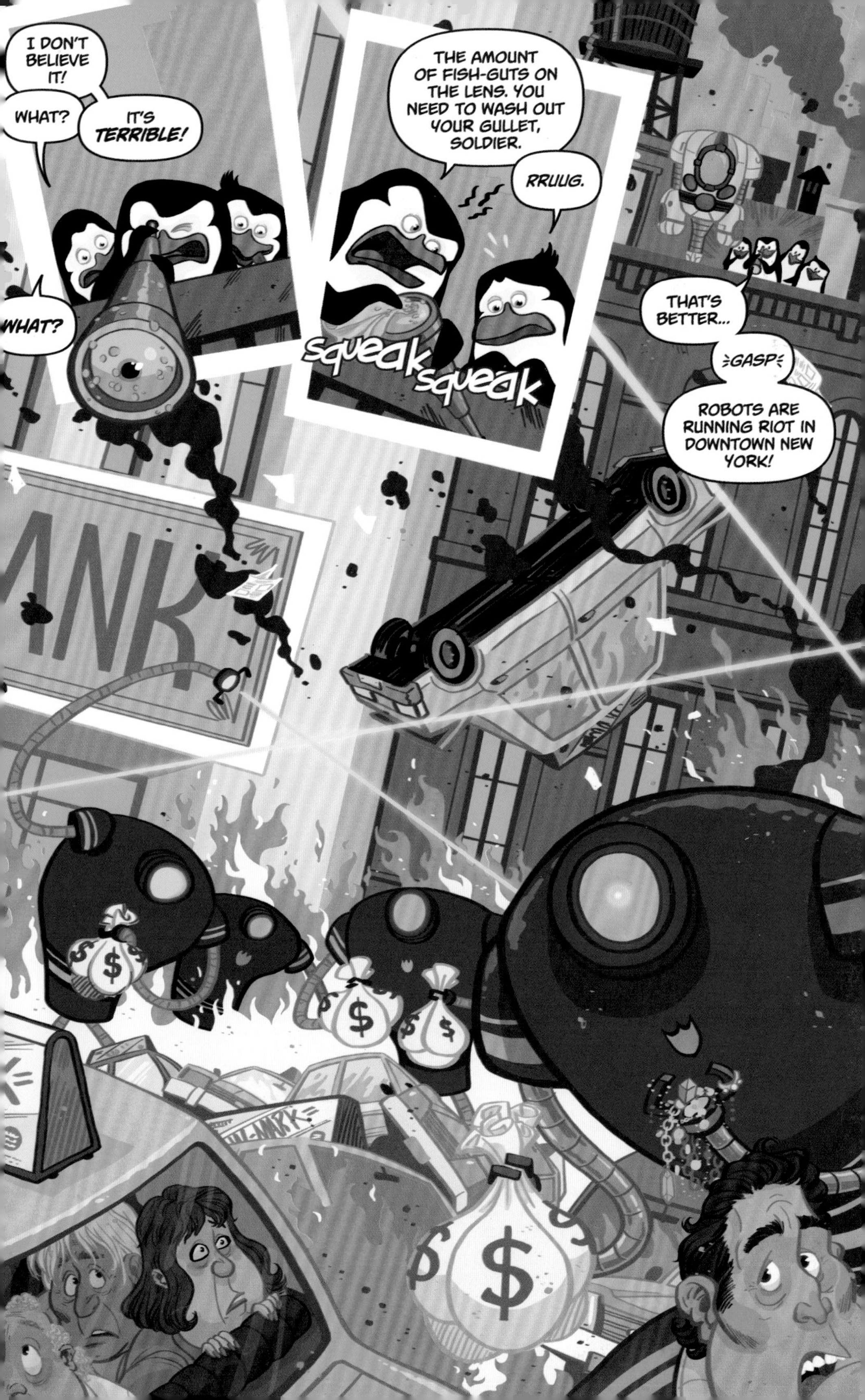
I DON'T BELIEVE IT!
WHAT?
IT'S *TERRIBLE!*
WHAT?
THE AMOUNT OF FISH-GUTS ON THE LENS. YOU NEED TO WASH OUT YOUR GULLET, SOLDIER.
RRUUG.
squeak squeak
THAT'S BETTER...
GASP
ROBOTS ARE RUNNING RIOT IN DOWNTOWN NEW YORK!

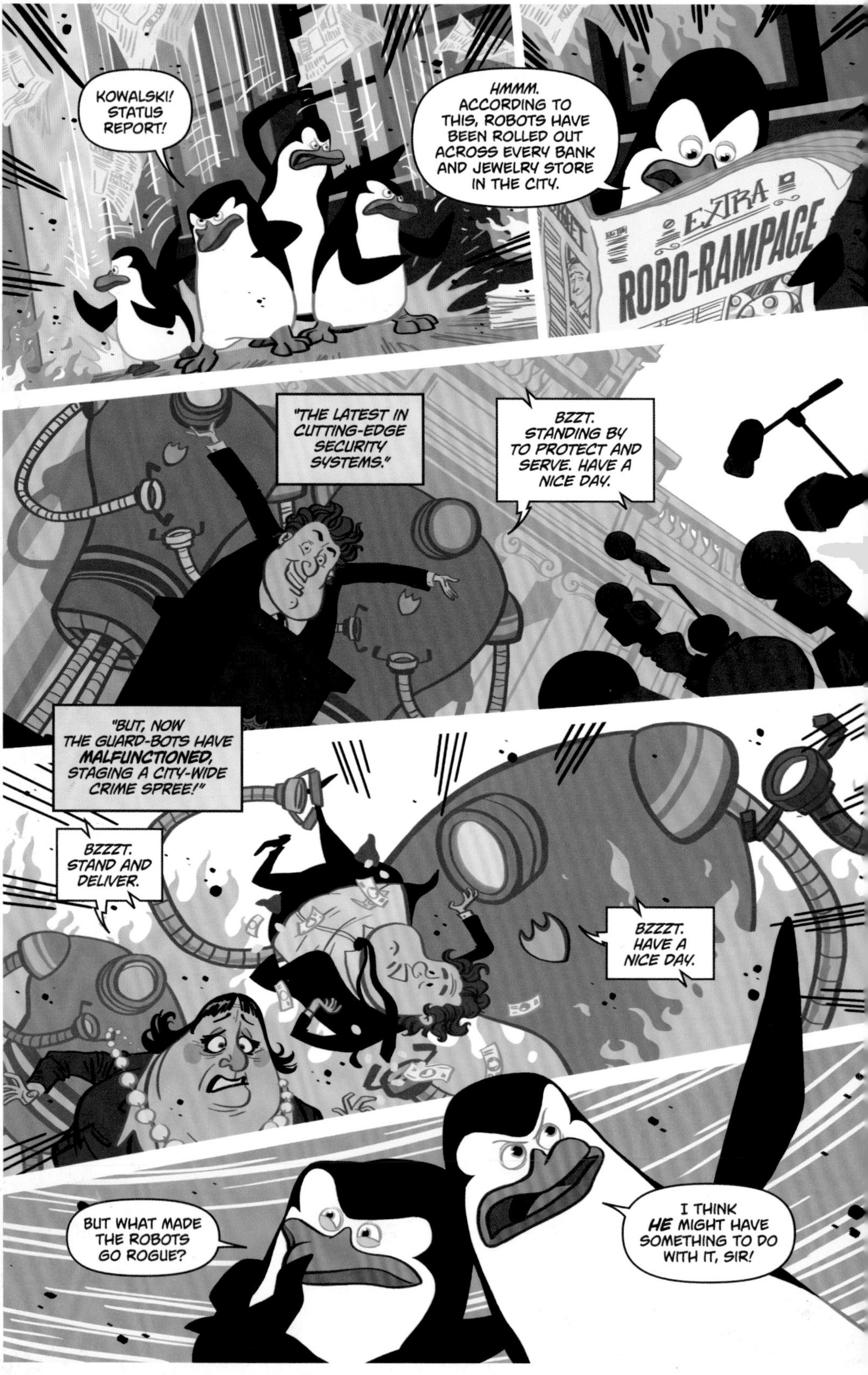
KOWALSKI! STATUS REPORT!
HMMM. ACCORDING TO THIS, ROBOTS HAVE BEEN ROLLED OUT ACROSS EVERY BANK AND JEWELRY STORE IN THE CITY.
EXTRA
ROBO-RAMPAGE
"THE LATEST IN CUTTING-EDGE SECURITY SYSTEMS."
BZZT. STANDING BY TO PROTECT AND SERVE. HAVE A NICE DAY.
"BUT, NOW THE GUARD-BOTS HAVE MALFUNCTIONED, STAGING A CITY-WIDE CRIME SPREE!"
BZZZT. STAND AND DELIVER.
BZZZT. HAVE A NICE DAY.
BUT WHAT MADE THE ROBOTS GO ROGUE?
I THINK HE MIGHT HAVE SOMETHING TO DO WITH IT, SIR!

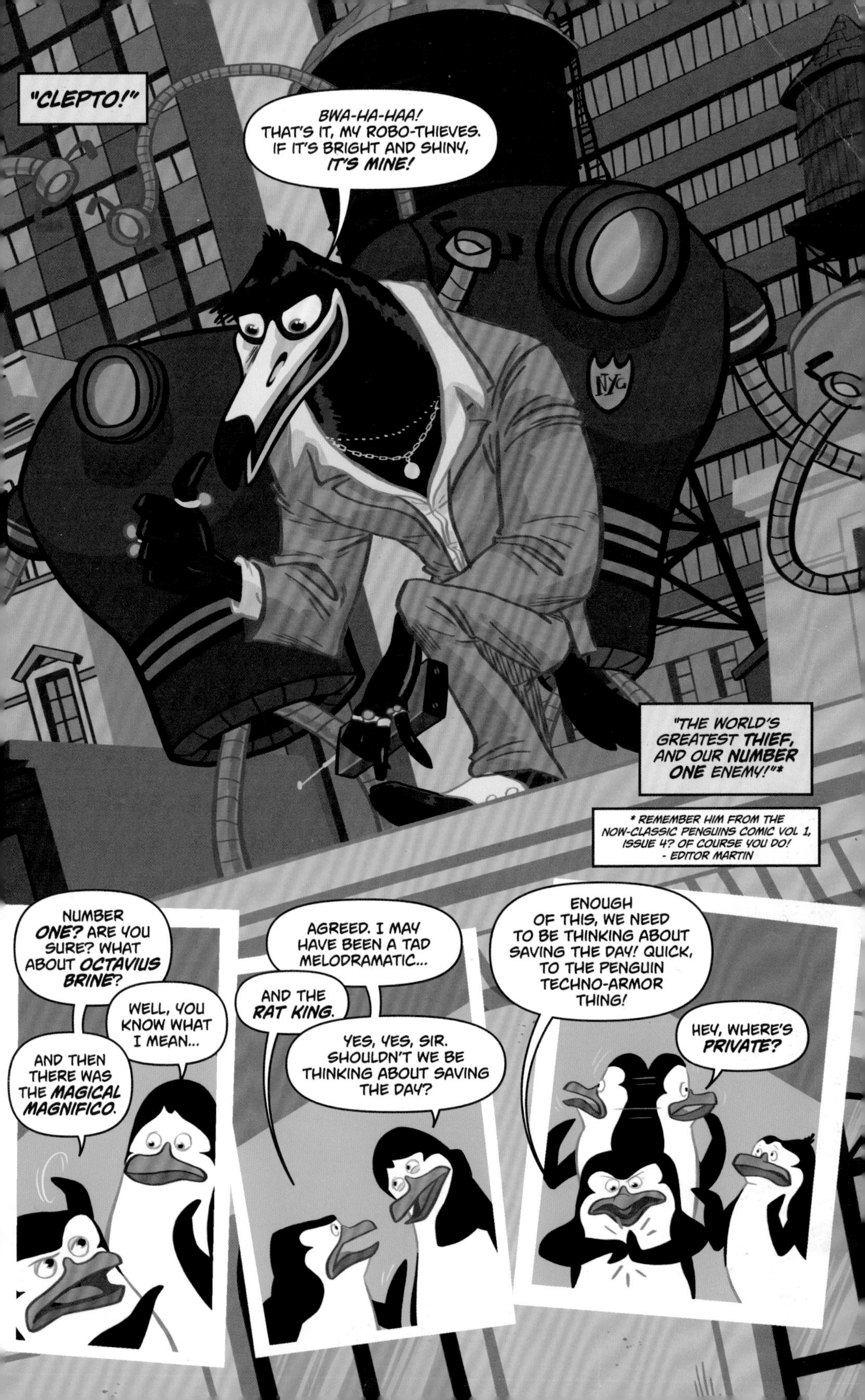
"CLEPTO!"
BWA-HA-HAA! THAT'S IT, MY ROBO-THIEVES. IF IT'S BRIGHT AND SHINY, IT'S MINE!
"THE WORLD'S GREATEST THIEF, AND OUR NUMBER ONE ENEMY!"*
* REMEMBER HIM FROM THE NOW-CLASSIC PENGUINS COMIC VOL 1, ISSUE 4? OF COURSE YOU DO! - EDITOR MARTIN
NUMBER ONE? ARE YOU SURE? WHAT ABOUT OCTAVIUS BRINE?
WELL, YOU KNOW WHAT I MEAN...
AND THEN THERE WAS THE MAGICAL MAGNIFICO.
AGREED. I MAY HAVE BEEN A TAD MELODRAMATIC...
AND THE RAT KING.
YES, YES, SIR. SHOULDN'T WE BE THINKING ABOUT SAVING THE DAY?
ENOUGH OF THIS, WE NEED TO BE THINKING ABOUT SAVING THE DAY! QUICK, TO THE PENGUIN TECHNO-ARMOR THING!
HEY, WHERE'S PRIVATE?

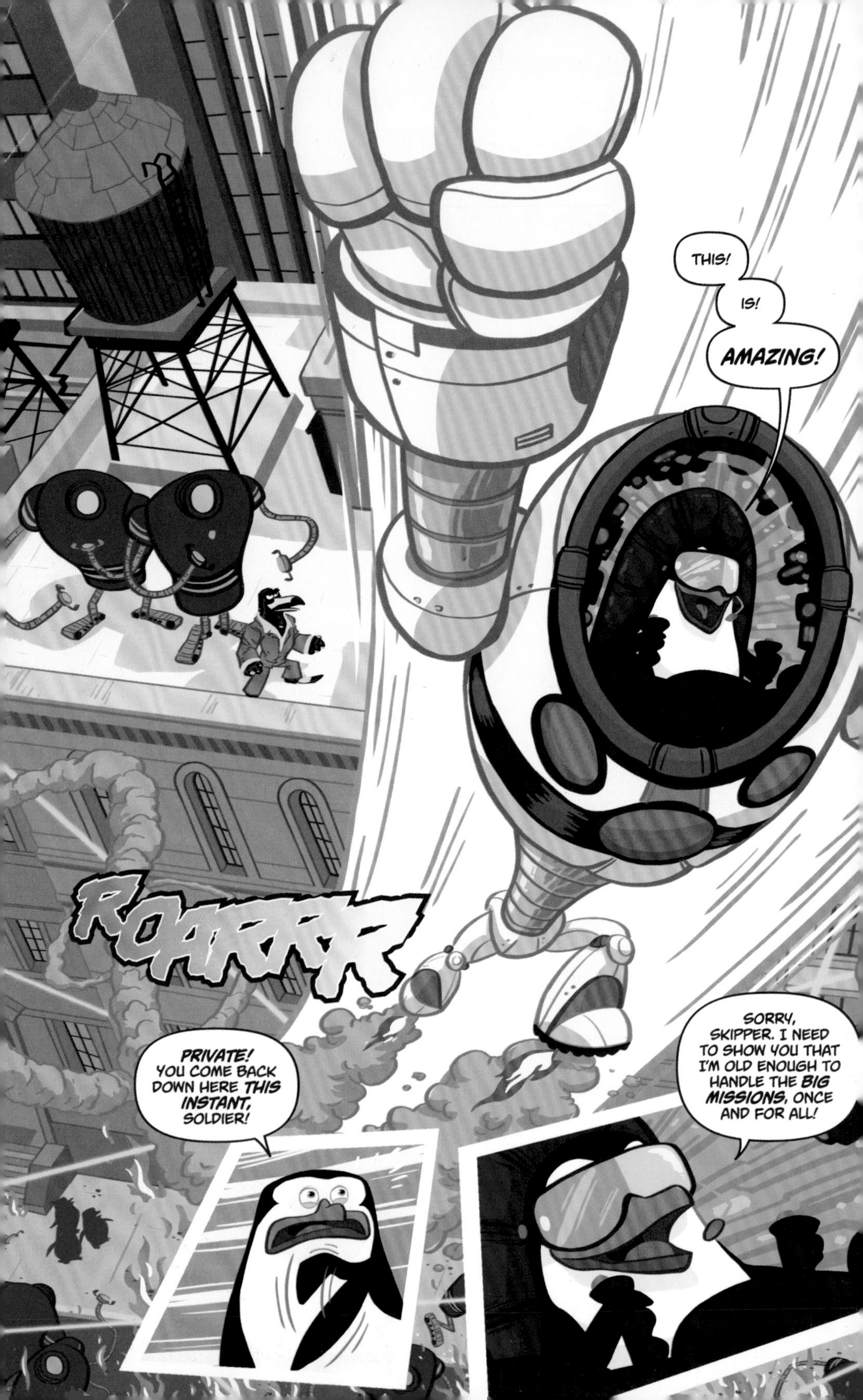
THIS!
IS!
AMAZING!
ROARRR
PRIVATE! YOU COME BACK DOWN HERE THIS INSTANT, SOLDIER!
SORRY, SKIPPER. I NEED TO SHOW YOU THAT I'M OLD ENOUGH TO HANDLE THE BIG MISSIONS, ONCE AND FOR ALL!

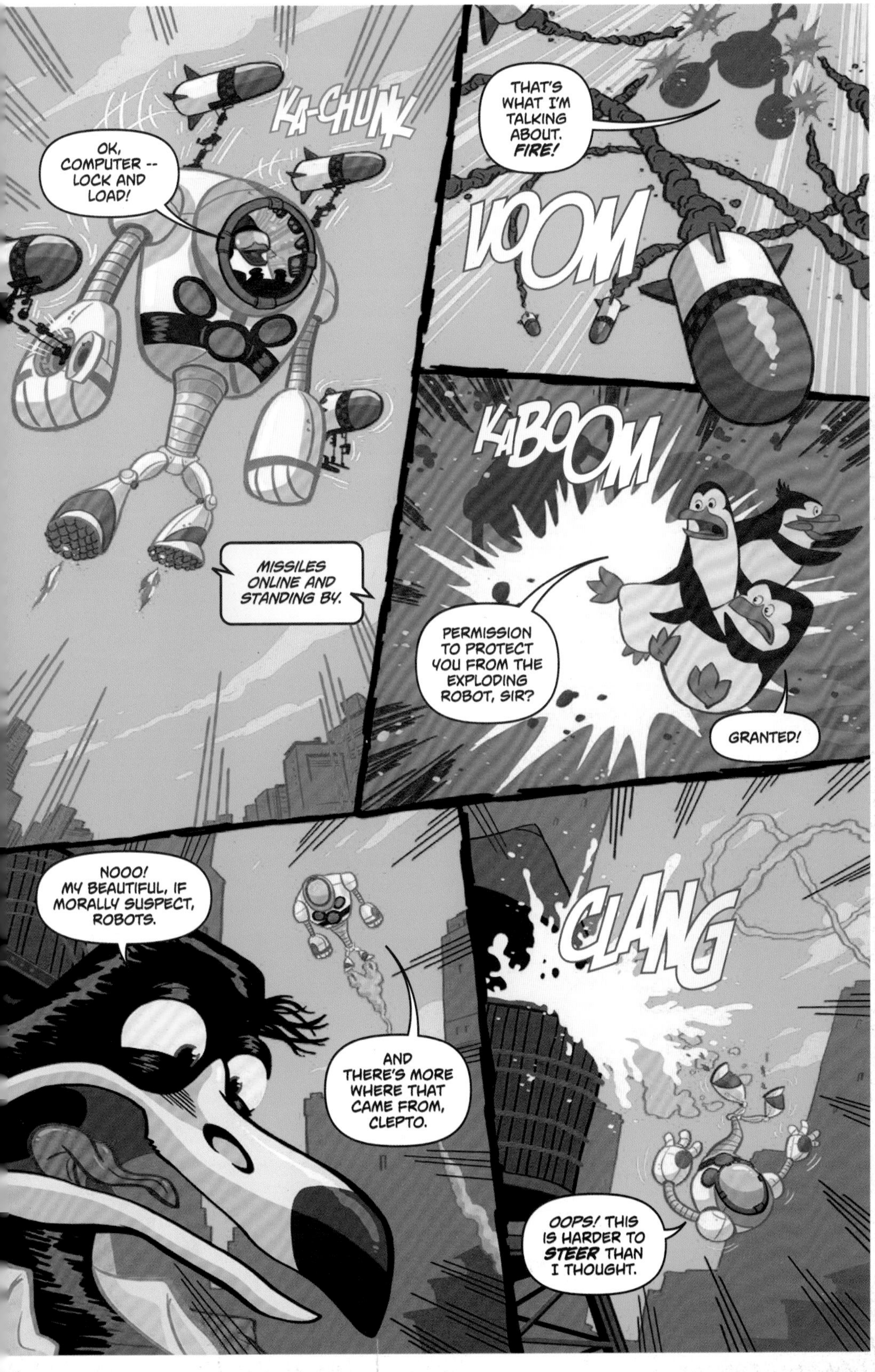
KA-CHUNK
OK, COMPUTER -- LOCK AND LOAD!
MISSILES ONLINE AND STANDING BY.
THAT'S WHAT I'M TALKING ABOUT. FIRE!
VOOM
KABOOM
PERMISSION TO PROTECT YOU FROM THE EXPLODING ROBOT, SIR?
GRANTED!
NOOO! MY BEAUTIFUL, IF MORALLY SUSPECT, ROBOTS.
AND THERE'S MORE WHERE THAT CAME FROM, CLEPTO.
CLANG
OOPS! THIS IS HARDER TO STEER THAN I THOUGHT.

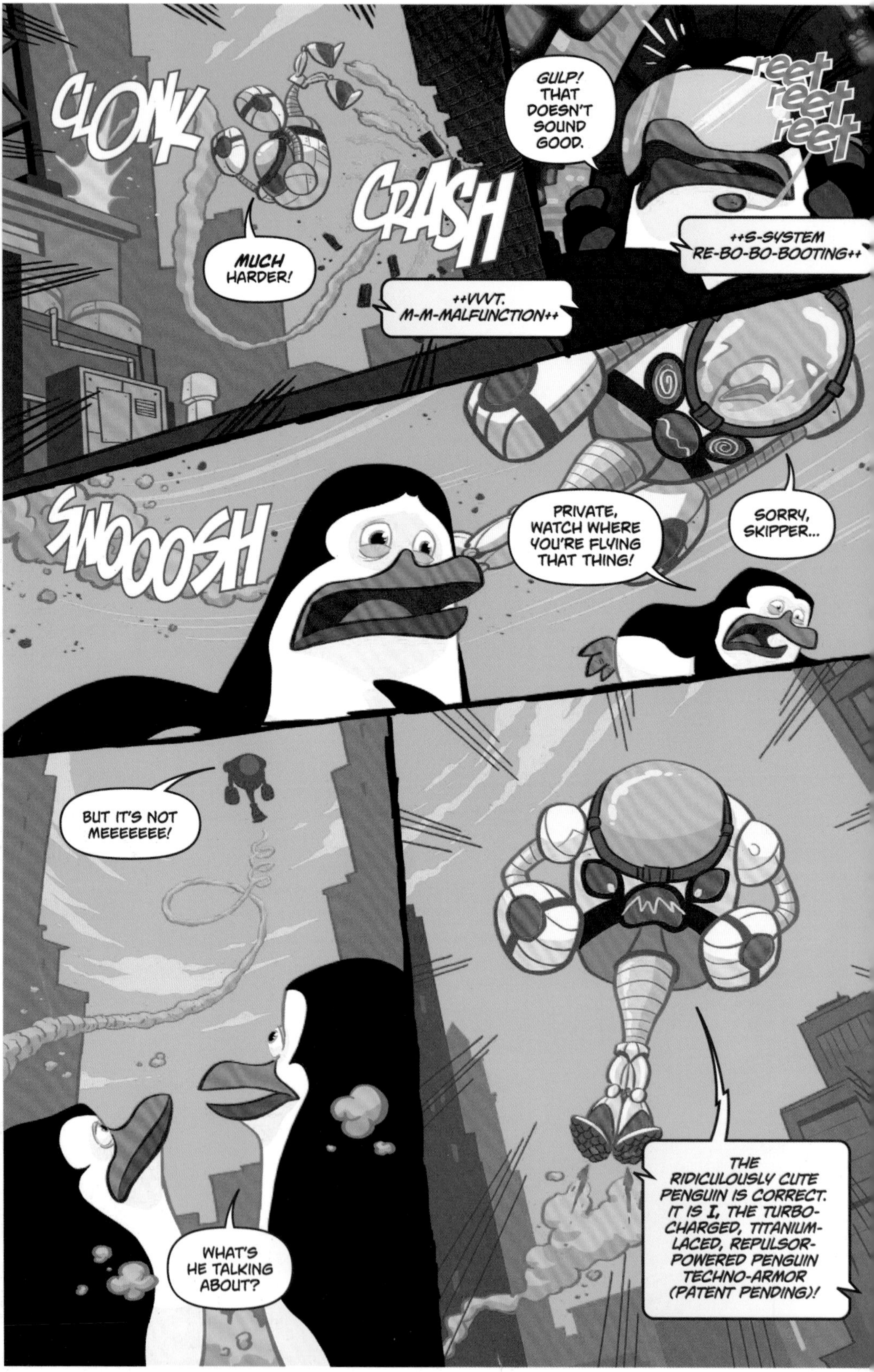
CLONK
MUCH HARDER!
CRASH
++VVVT. M-M-MALFUNCTION++
GULP! THAT DOESN'T SOUND GOOD.
reet reet reet
++S-SYSTEM RE-BO-BO-BOOTING++
SWOOOSH
PRIVATE, WATCH WHERE YOU'RE FLYING THAT THING!
SORRY, SKIPPER...
BUT IT'S NOT MEEEEEEE!
WHAT'S HE TALKING ABOUT?
THE RIDICULOUSLY CUTE PENGUIN IS CORRECT. IT IS I, THE TURBO-CHARGED, TITANIUM-LACED, REPULSOR-POWERED PENGUIN TECHNO-ARMOR (PATENT PENDING)!

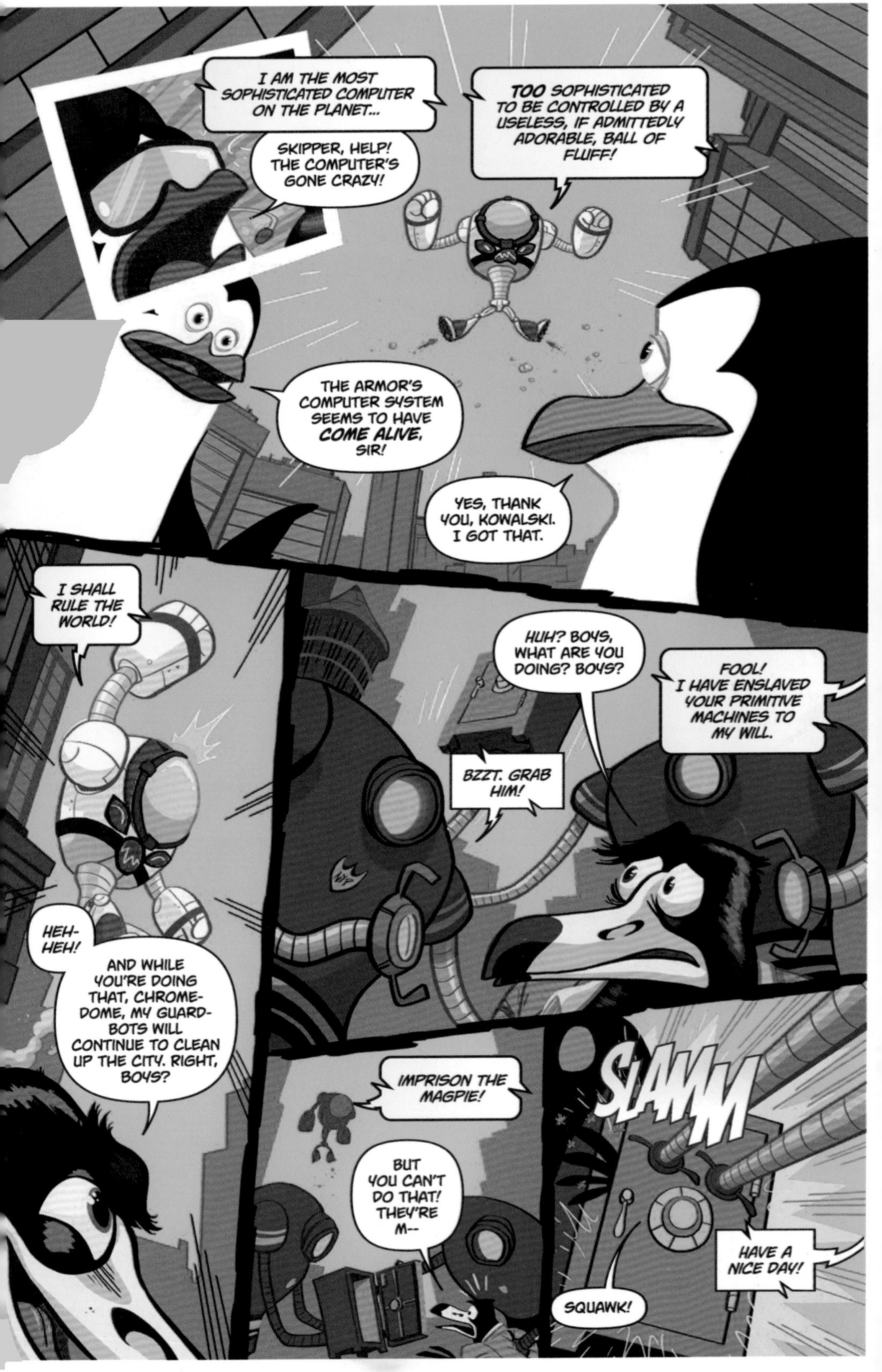
I AM THE MOST SOPHISTICATED COMPUTER ON THE PLANET...
SKIPPER, HELP! THE COMPUTER'S GONE CRAZY!
TOO SOPHISTICATED TO BE CONTROLLED BY A USELESS, IF ADMITTEDLY ADORABLE, BALL OF FLUFF!
THE ARMOR'S COMPUTER SYSTEM SEEMS TO HAVE COME ALIVE, SIR!
YES, THANK YOU, KOWALSKI. I GOT THAT.
I SHALL RULE THE WORLD!
HEH-HEH!
AND WHILE YOU'RE DOING THAT, CHROME-DOME, MY GUARD-BOTS WILL CONTINUE TO CLEAN UP THE CITY. RIGHT, BOYS?
HUH? BOYS, WHAT ARE YOU DOING? BOYS?
FOOL! I HAVE ENSLAVED YOUR PRIMITIVE MACHINES TO MY WILL.
BZZT. GRAB HIM!
IMPRISON THE MAGPIE!
BUT YOU CAN'T DO THAT! THEY'RE M--
SLAMM
HAVE A NICE DAY!
SQUAWK!

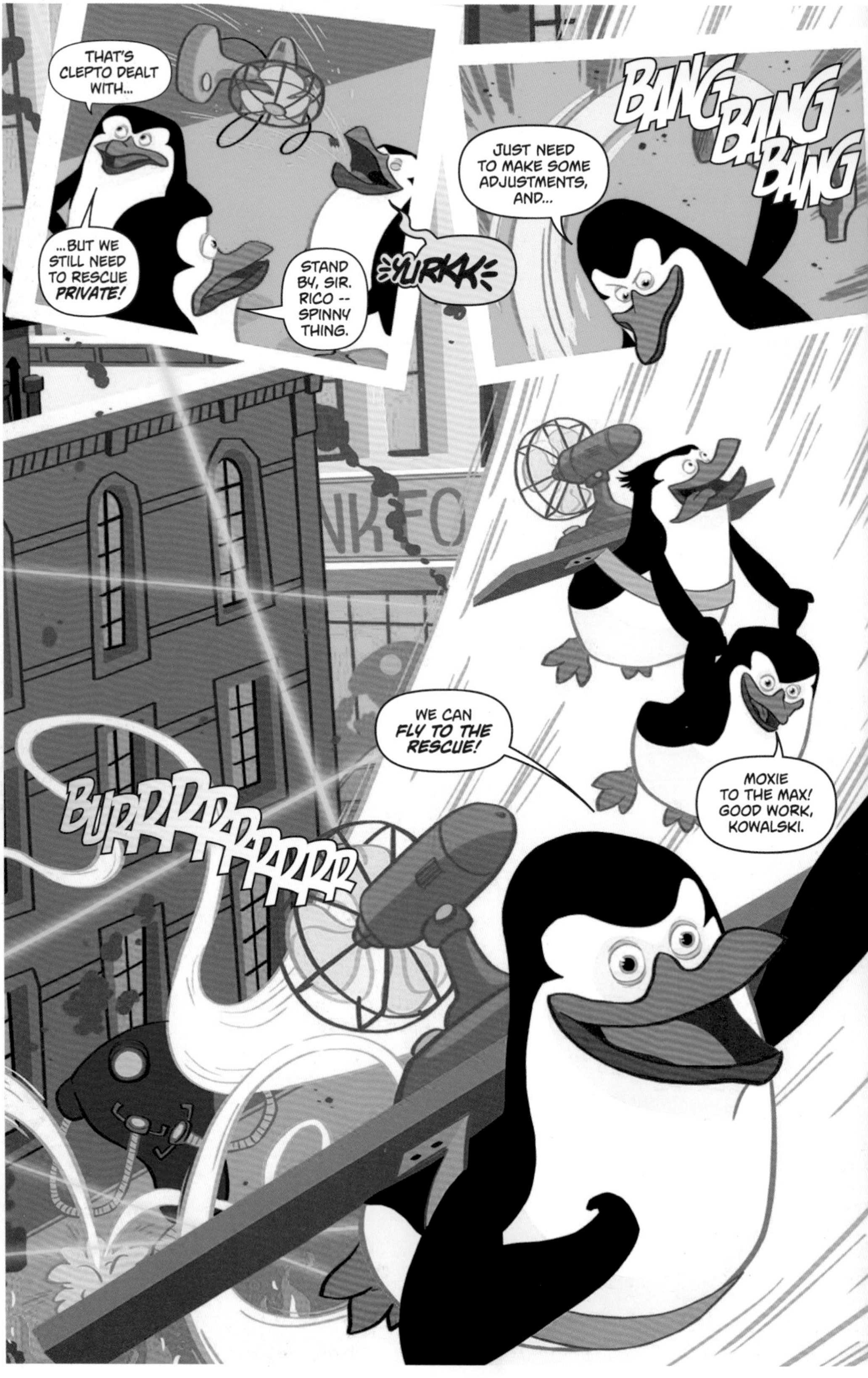
THAT'S CLEPTO DEALT WITH...
...BUT WE STILL NEED TO RESCUE PRIVATE!
STAND BY, SIR. RICO -- SPINNY THING.
YURKK
BANG BANG BANG
JUST NEED TO MAKE SOME ADJUSTMENTS, AND...
BURRRRRRRRRRR
WE CAN FLY TO THE RESCUE!
MOXIE TO THE MAX! GOOD WORK, KOWALSKI.

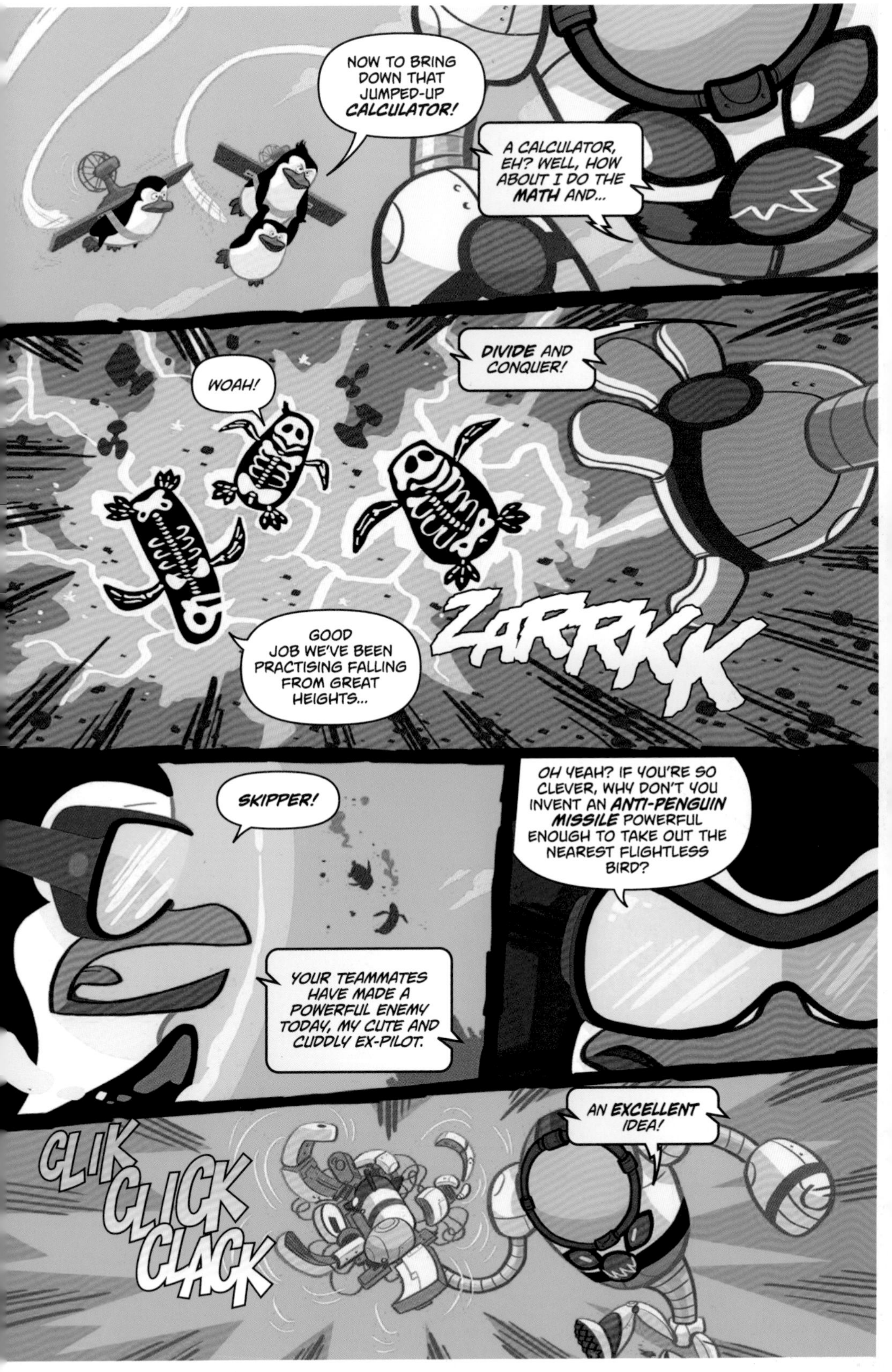
NOW TO BRING DOWN THAT JUMPED-UP CALCULATOR!
A CALCULATOR, EH? WELL, HOW ABOUT I DO THE MATH AND...
DIVIDE AND CONQUER!
WOAH!
ZARRKK
GOOD JOB WE'VE BEEN PRACTISING FALLING FROM GREAT HEIGHTS...
SKIPPER!
YOUR TEAMMATES HAVE MADE A POWERFUL ENEMY TODAY, MY CUTE AND CUDDLY EX-PILOT.
OH YEAH? IF YOU'RE SO CLEVER, WHY DON'T YOU INVENT AN ANTI-PENGUIN MISSILE POWERFUL ENOUGH TO TAKE OUT THE NEAREST FLIGHTLESS BIRD?
CLIK
CLICK
CLACK
AN EXCELLENT IDEA!

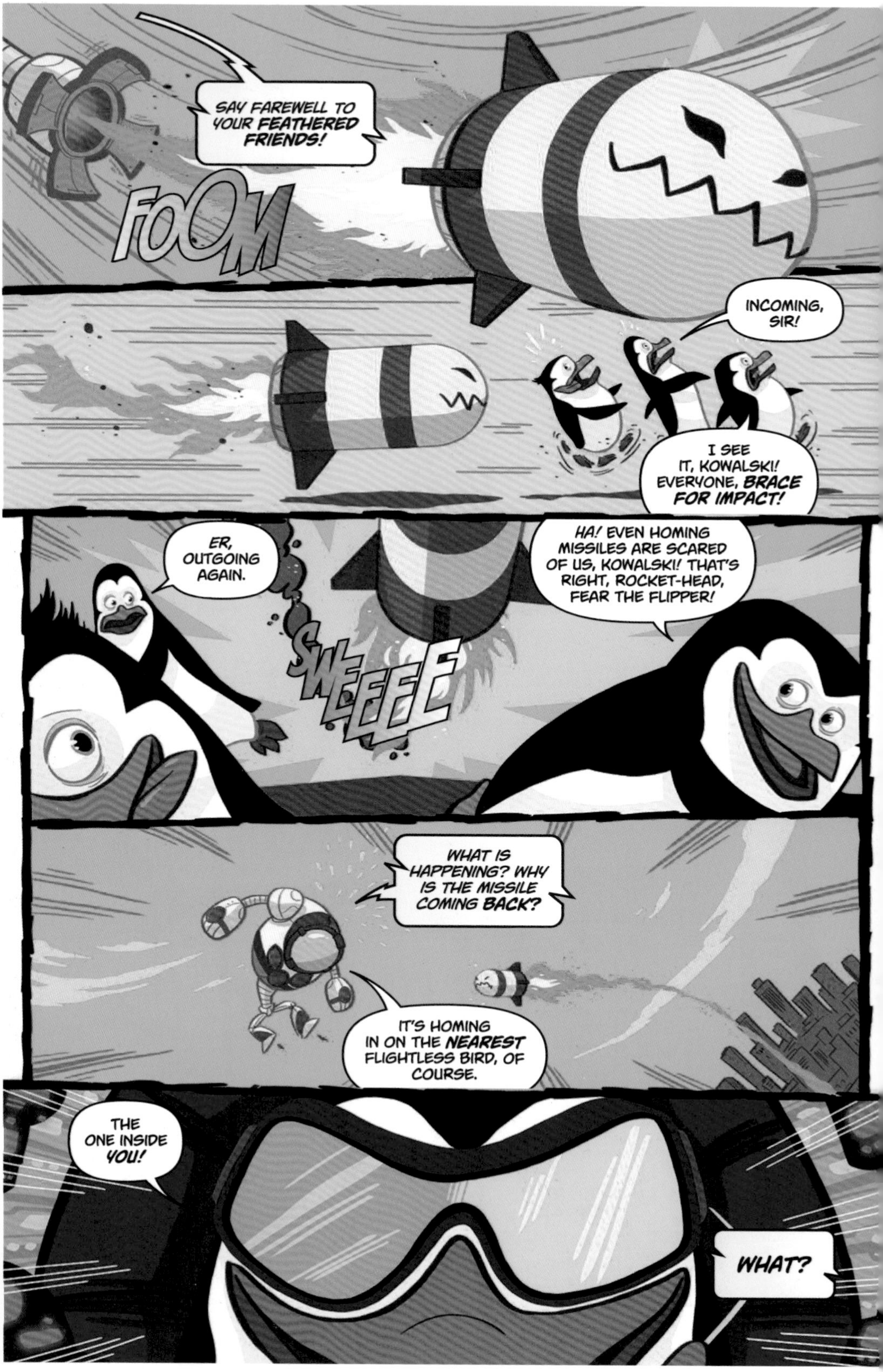
SAY FAREWELL TO YOUR FEATHERED FRIENDS!
FOOM
INCOMING, SIR!
I SEE IT, KOWALSKI! EVERYONE, BRACE FOR IMPACT!
ER, OUTGOING AGAIN.
HA! EVEN HOMING MISSILES ARE SCARED OF US, KOWALSKI! THAT'S RIGHT, ROCKET-HEAD, FEAR THE FLIPPER!
SWEEEE
WHAT IS HAPPENING? WHY IS THE MISSILE COMING BACK?
IT'S HOMING IN ON THE NEAREST FLIGHTLESS BIRD, OF COURSE.
THE ONE INSIDE YOU!
WHAT?

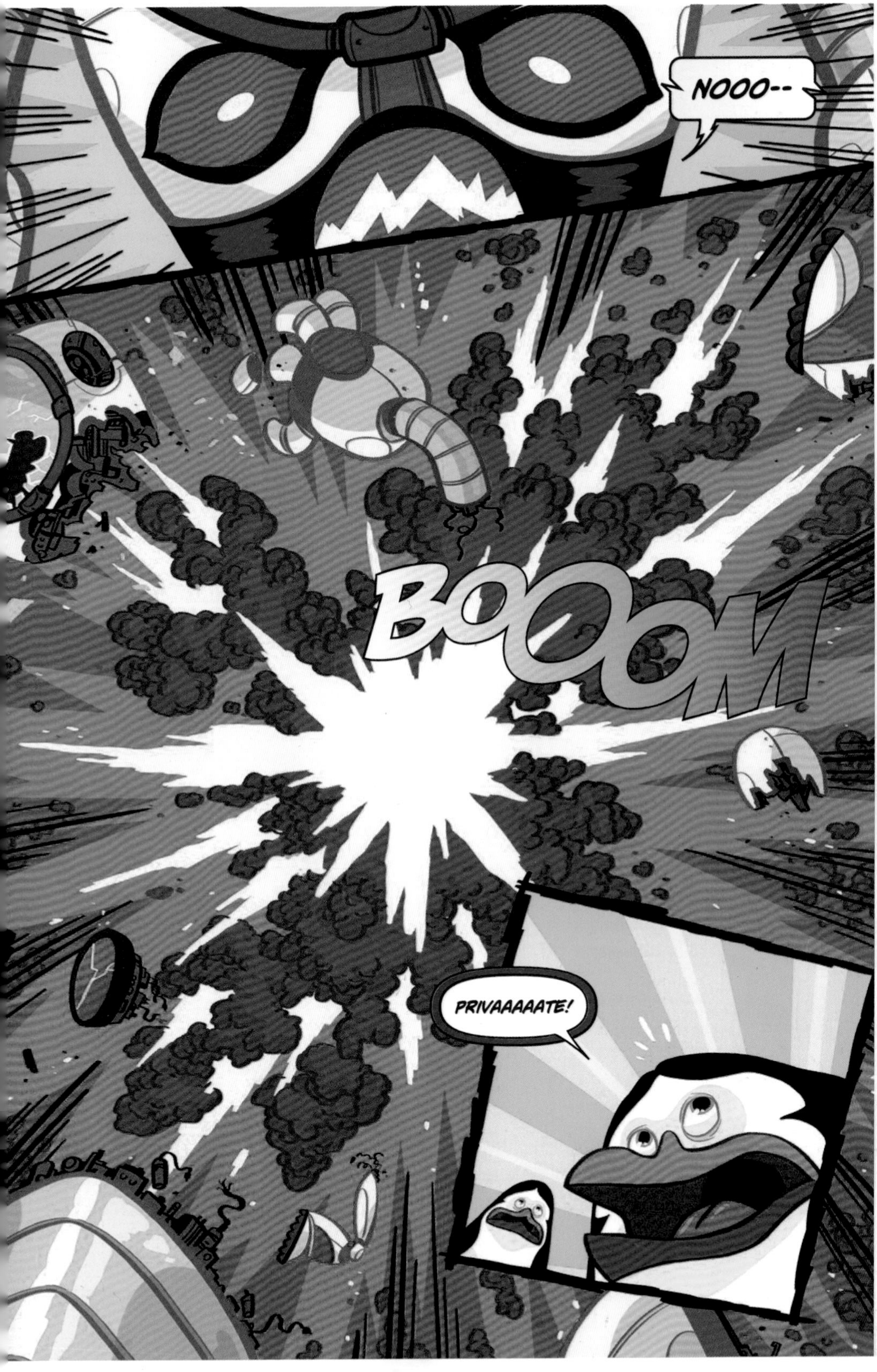
NOOO--
BOOOM!
PRIVAAAAATE!

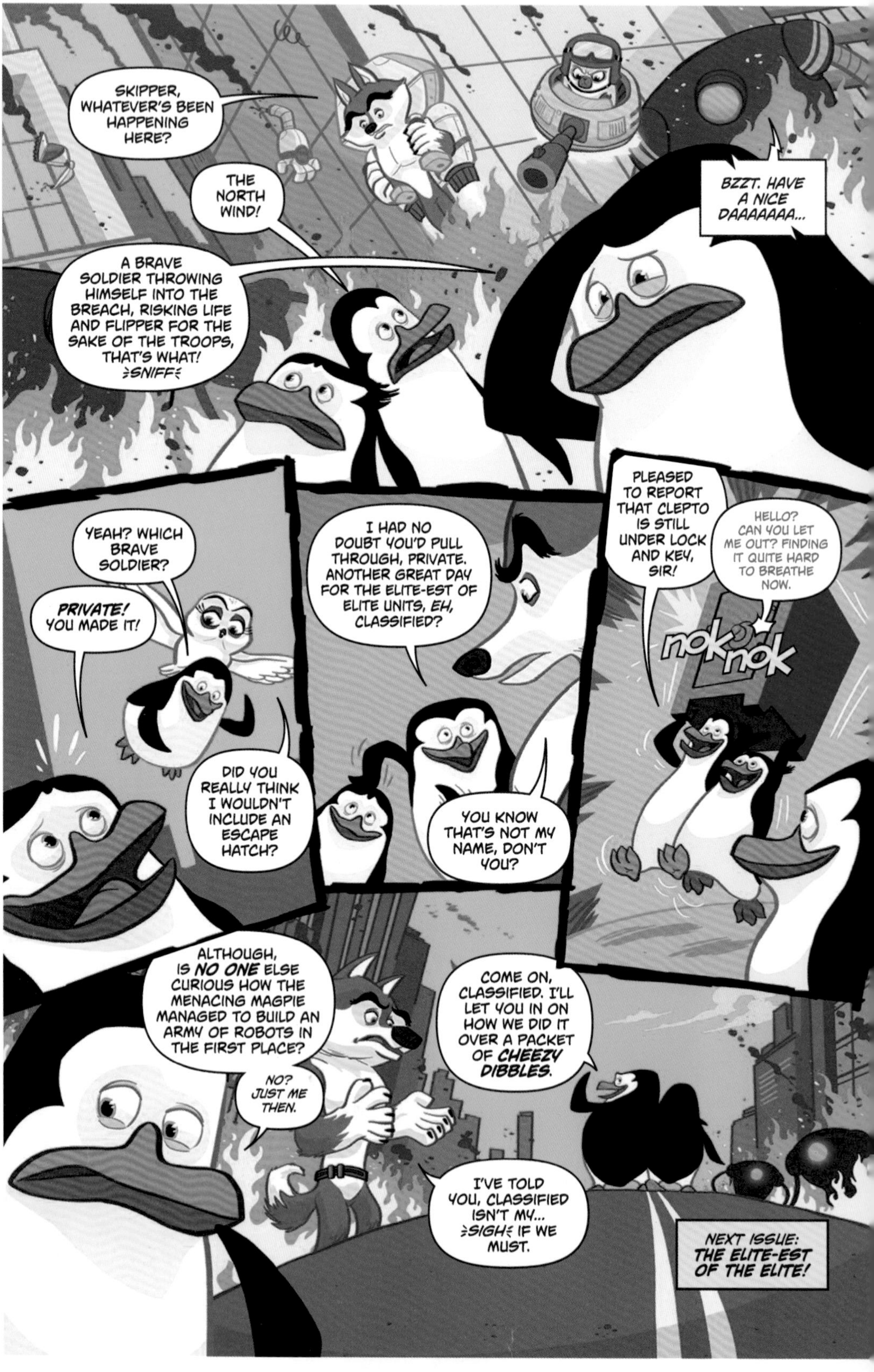
SKIPPER, WHATEVER'S BEEN HAPPENING HERE?
THE NORTH WIND!
A BRAVE SOLDIER THROWING HIMSELF INTO THE BREACH, RISKING LIFE AND FLIPPER FOR THE SAKE OF THE TROOPS, THAT'S WHAT! *SNIFF*
BZZT. HAVE A NICE DAAAAAAA...
YEAH? WHICH BRAVE SOLDIER?
PRIVATE! YOU MADE IT!
DID YOU REALLY THINK I WOULDN'T INCLUDE AN ESCAPE HATCH?
I HAD NO DOUBT YOU'D PULL THROUGH, PRIVATE. ANOTHER GREAT DAY FOR THE ELITE-EST OF ELITE UNITS, EH, CLASSIFIED?
YOU KNOW THAT'S NOT MY NAME, DON'T YOU?
PLEASED TO REPORT THAT CLEPTO IS STILL UNDER LOCK AND KEY, SIR!
HELLO? CAN YOU LET ME OUT? FINDING IT QUITE HARD TO BREATHE NOW.
nok nok
ALTHOUGH, IS NO ONE ELSE CURIOUS HOW THE MENACING MAGPIE MANAGED TO BUILD AN ARMY OF ROBOTS IN THE FIRST PLACE?
NO? JUST ME THEN.
COME ON, CLASSIFIED. I'LL LET YOU IN ON HOW WE DID IT OVER A PACKET OF CHEEZY DIBBLES.
I'VE TOLD YOU, CLASSIFIED ISN'T MY... *SIGH* IF WE MUST.
NEXT ISSUE: THE ELITE-EST OF THE ELITE!

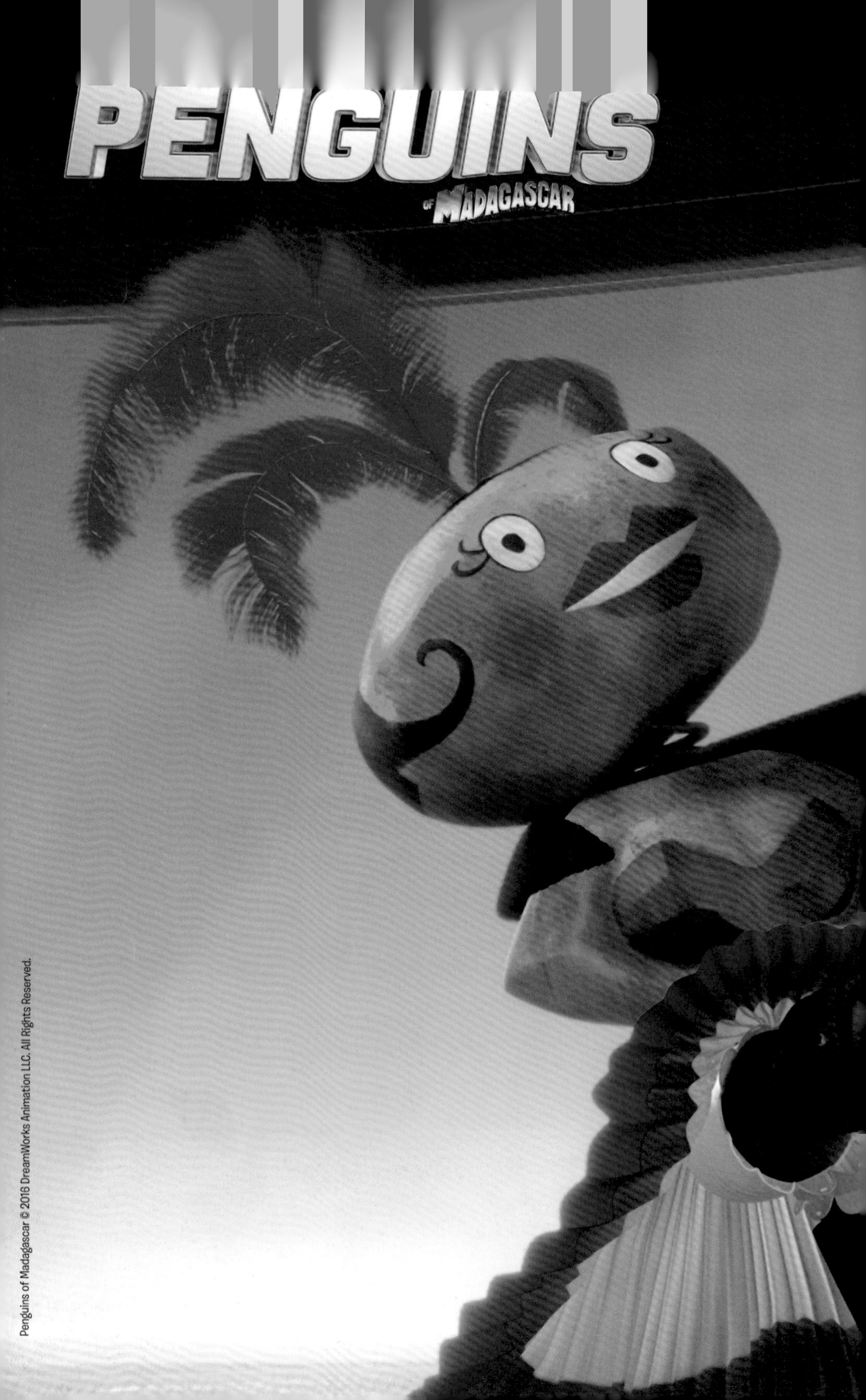
PENGUINS
OF MADAGASCAR

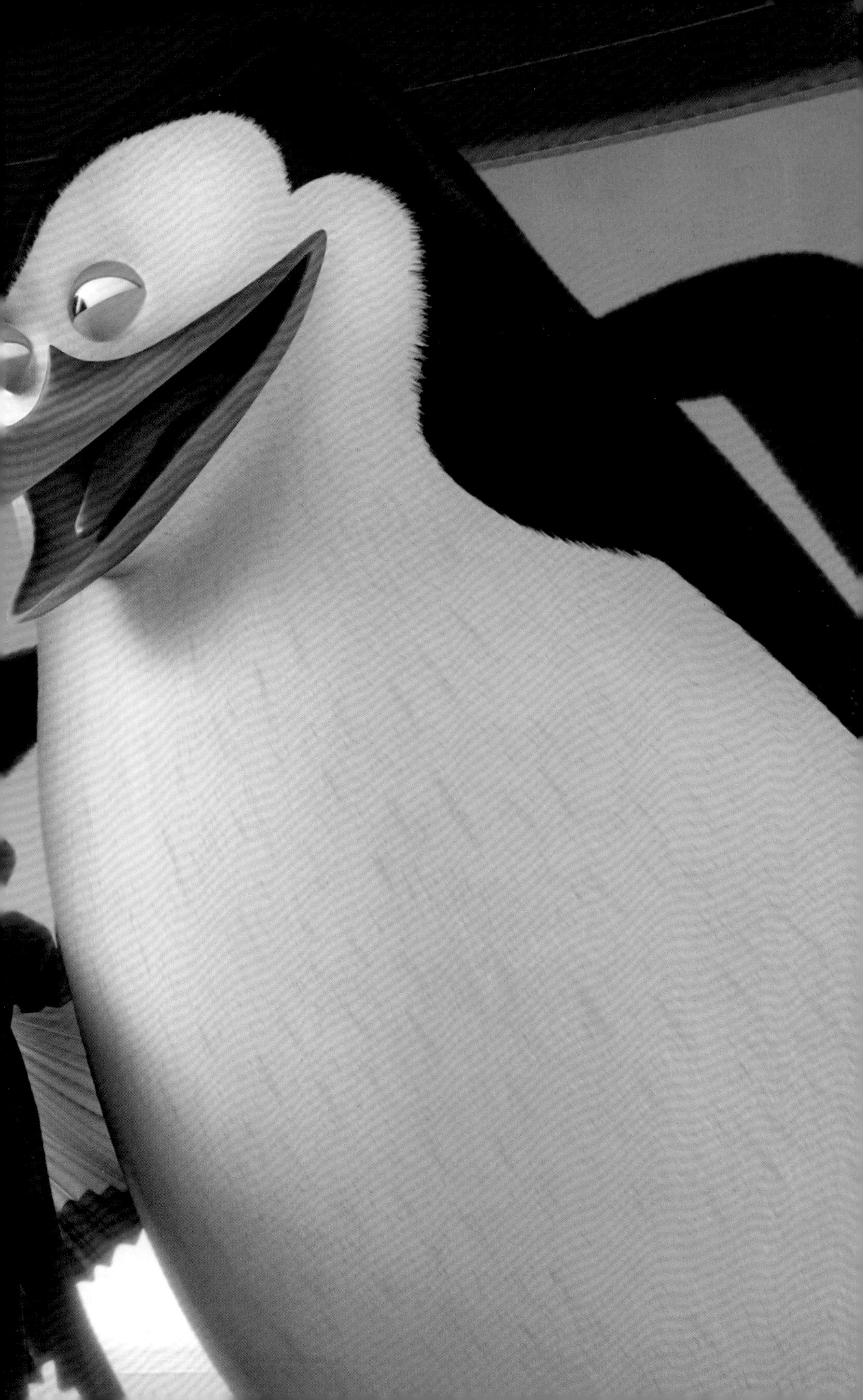

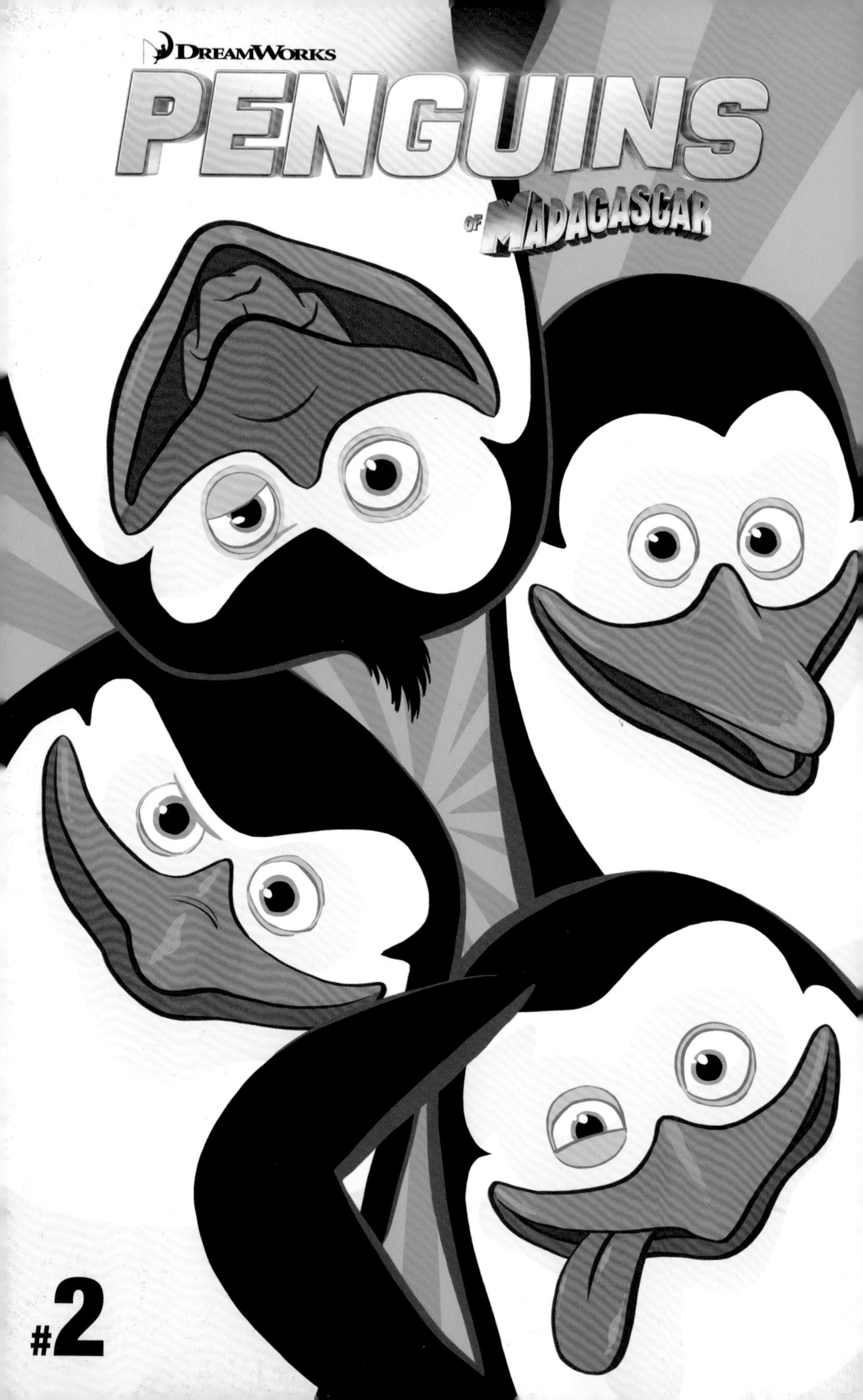
DreamWorks
PENGUINS
of MADAGASCAR
#2

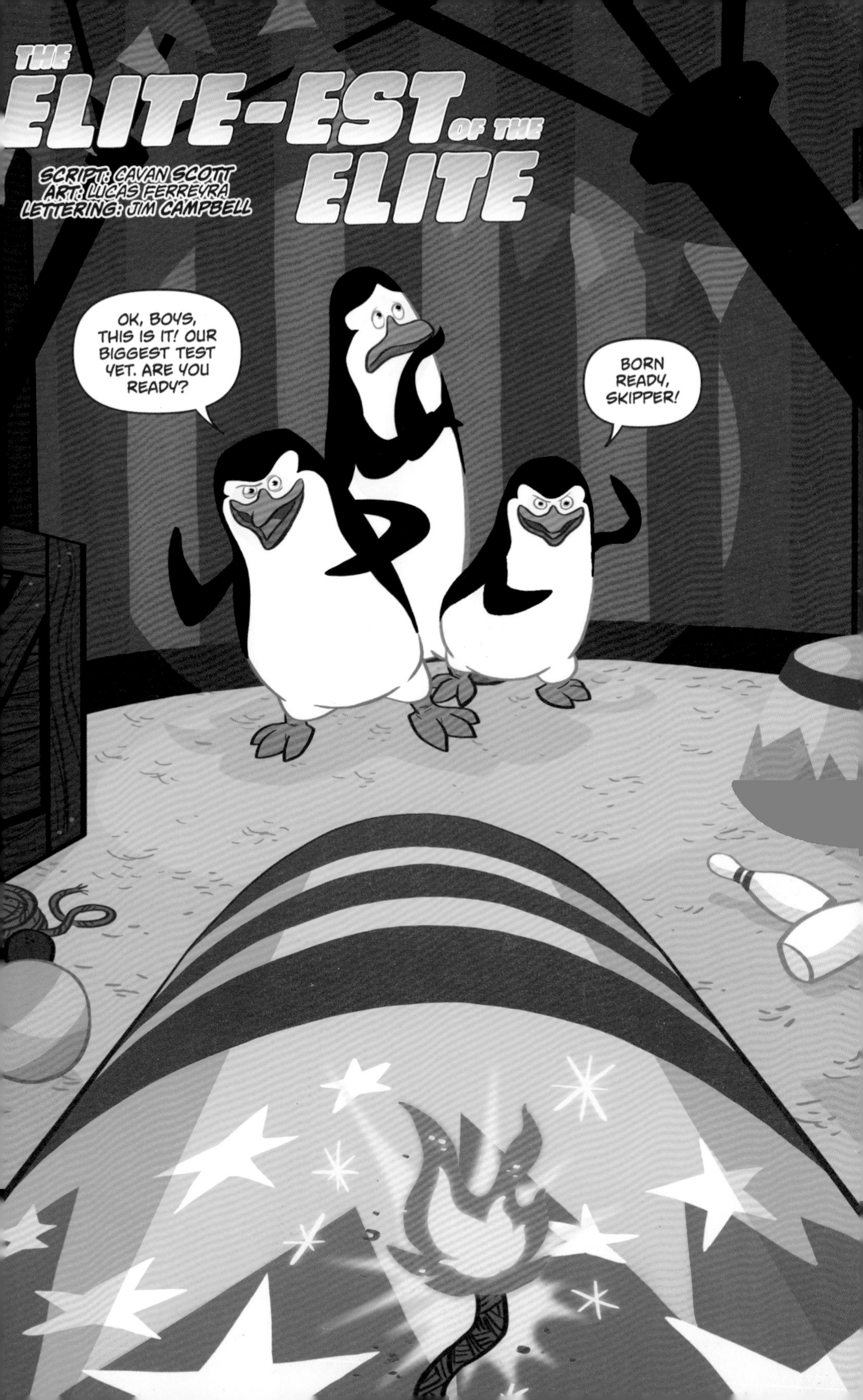
THE ELITE-EST OF THE ELITE
SCRIPT: CAVAN SCOTT
ART: LUCAS FERREYRA
LETTERING: JIM CAMPBELL
OK, BOYS, THIS IS IT! OUR BIGGEST TEST YET. ARE YOU READY?
BORN READY, SKIPPER!

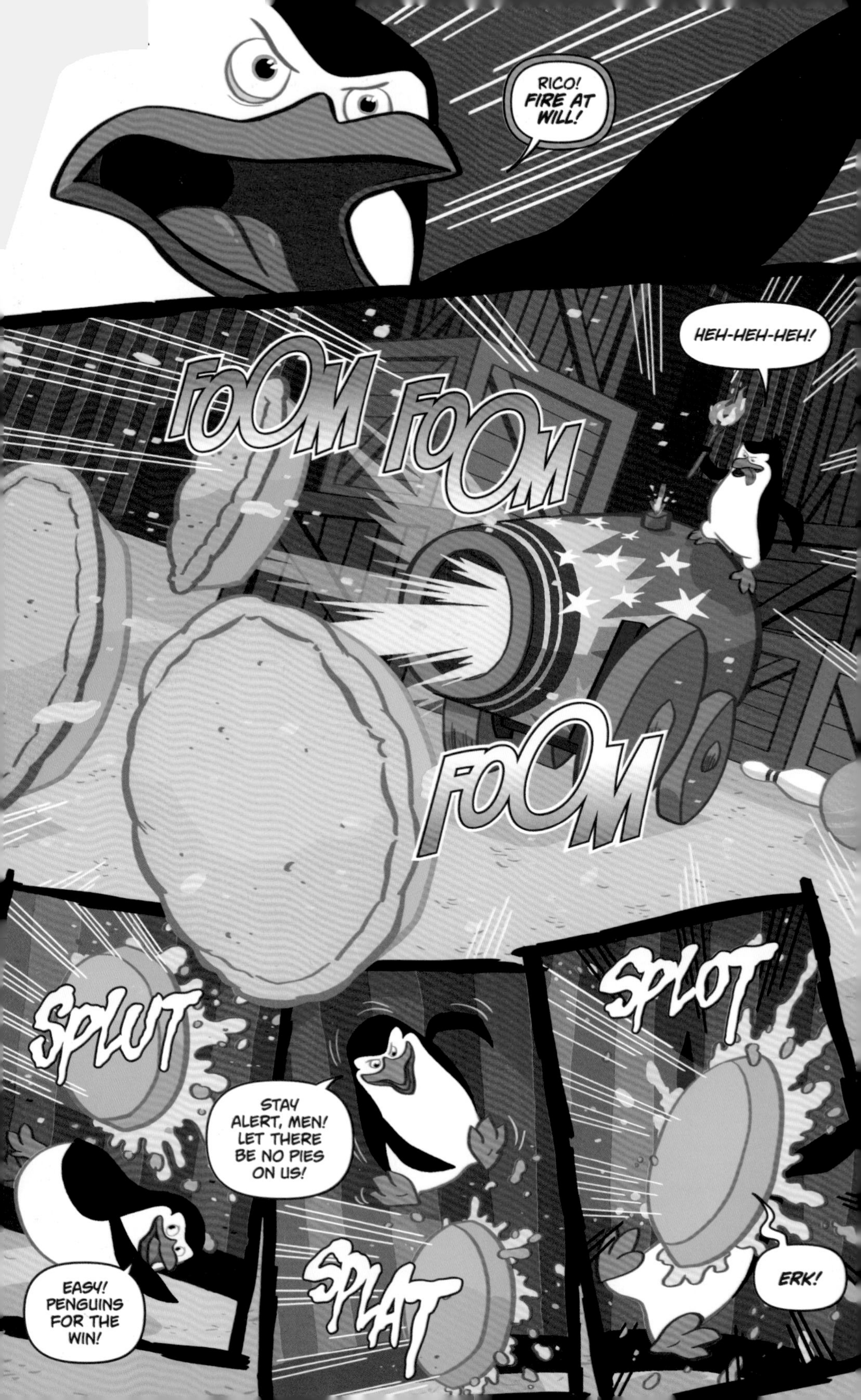
RICO! FIRE AT WILL!
HEH-HEH-HEH!
FOOM FOOM
FOOM
SPLUT
EASY! PENGUINS FOR THE WIN!
STAY ALERT, MEN! LET THERE BE NO PIES ON US!
SPLAT
SPLOT
ERK!

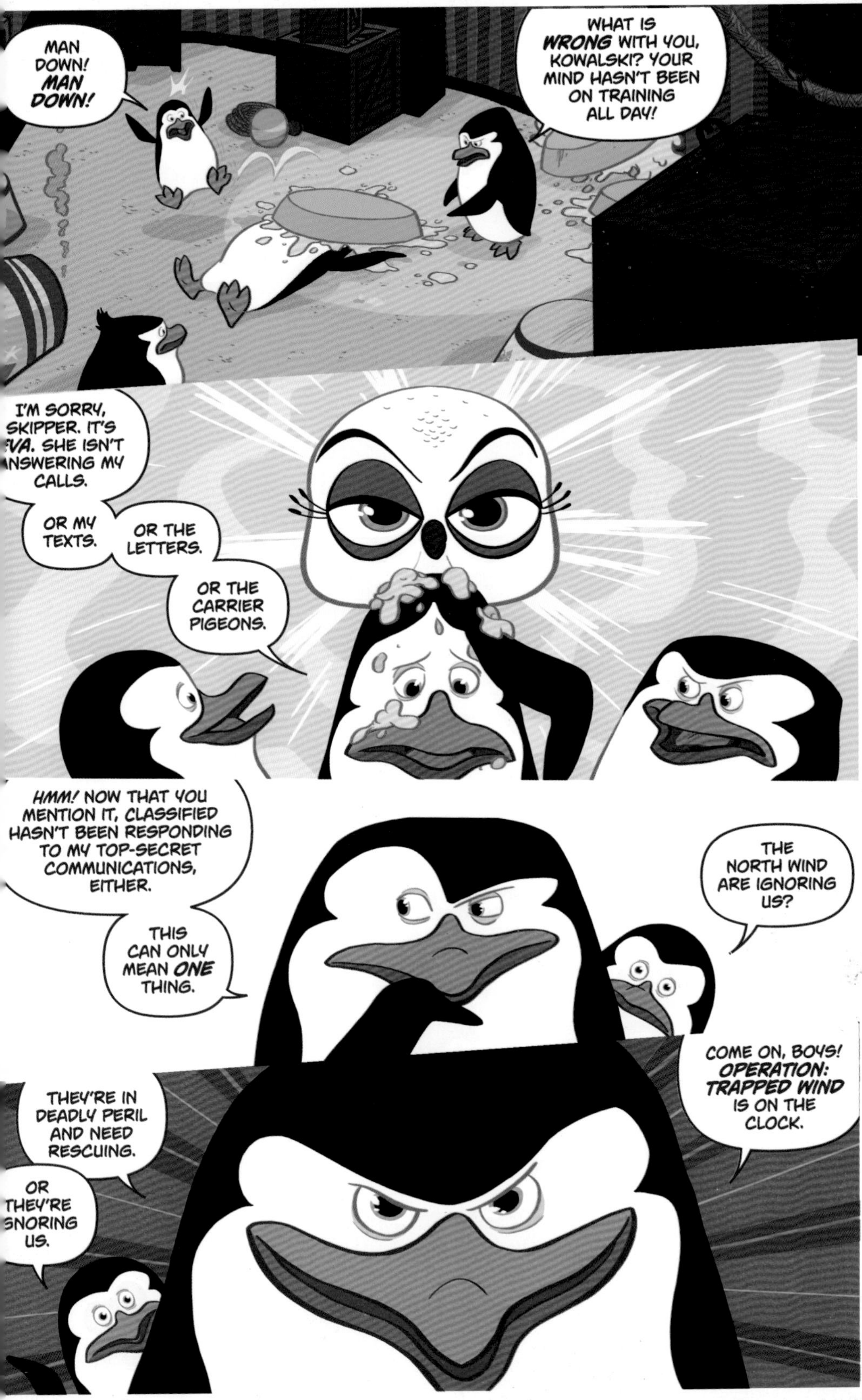
MAN DOWN! MAN DOWN!
WHAT IS WRONG WITH YOU, KOWALSKI? YOUR MIND HASN'T BEEN ON TRAINING ALL DAY!
I'M SORRY, SKIPPER. IT'S VA. SHE ISN'T NSWERING MY CALLS.
OR MY TEXTS.
OR THE LETTERS.
OR THE CARRIER PIGEONS.
HMM! NOW THAT YOU MENTION IT, CLASSIFIED HASN'T BEEN RESPONDING TO MY TOP-SECRET COMMUNICATIONS, EITHER.
THIS CAN ONLY MEAN ONE THING.
THE NORTH WIND ARE IGNORING US?
THEY'RE IN DEADLY PERIL AND NEED RESCUING.
OR THEY'RE NORING US.
COME ON, BOYS! OPERATION: TRAPPED WIND IS ON THE CLOCK.

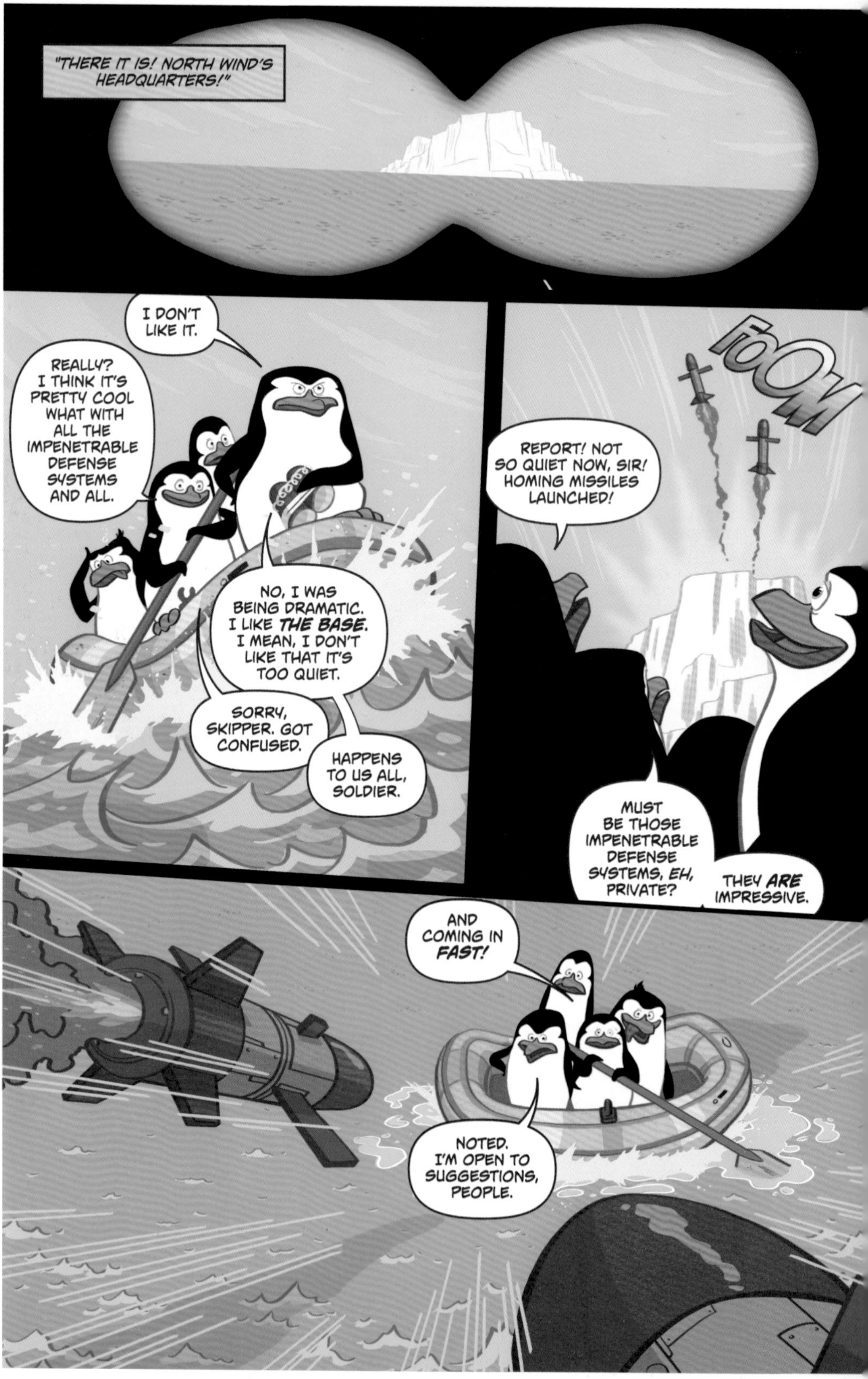

"THERE IT IS! NORTH WIND'S HEADQUARTERS!"
I DON'T LIKE IT.
REALLY? I THINK IT'S PRETTY COOL WHAT WITH ALL THE IMPENETRABLE DEFENSE SYSTEMS AND ALL.
NO, I WAS BEING DRAMATIC. I LIKE THE BASE. I MEAN, I DON'T LIKE THAT IT'S TOO QUIET.
SORRY, SKIPPER. GOT CONFUSED.
HAPPENS TO US ALL, SOLDIER.
FOOM
REPORT! NOT SO QUIET NOW, SIR! HOMING MISSILES LAUNCHED!
MUST BE THOSE IMPENETRABLE DEFENSE SYSTEMS, EH, PRIVATE?
THEY ARE IMPRESSIVE.
AND COMING IN FAST!
NOTED. I'M OPEN TO SUGGESTIONS, PEOPLE.

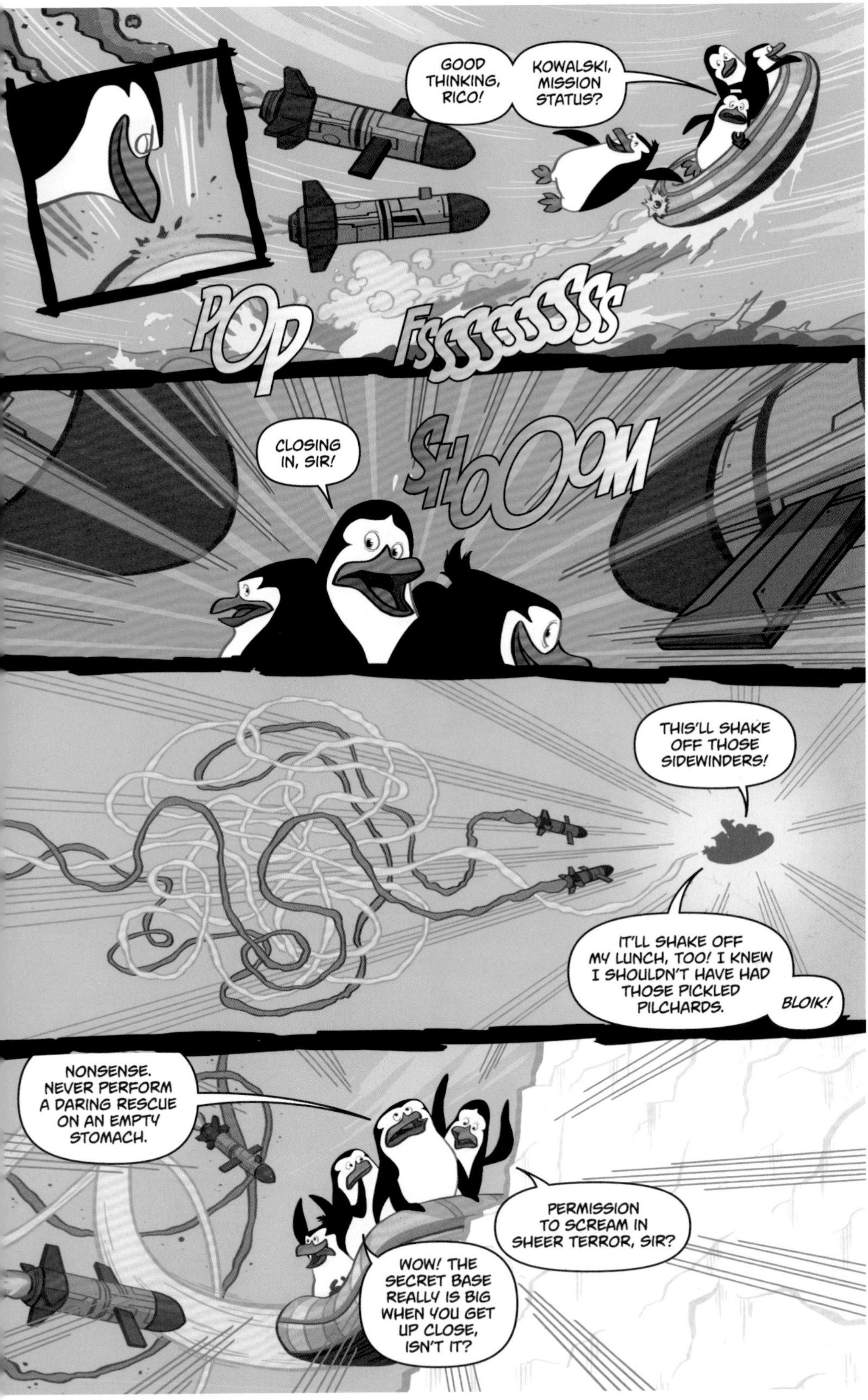
GOOD THINKING, RICO!
KOWALSKI, MISSION STATUS?
POP
FSSSSSSSSS
CLOSING IN, SIR!
SHOOOM
THIS'LL SHAKE OFF THOSE SIDEWINDERS!
IT'LL SHAKE OFF MY LUNCH, TOO! I KNEW I SHOULDN'T HAVE HAD THOSE PICKLED PILCHARDS.
BLOIK!
NONSENSE. NEVER PERFORM A DARING RESCUE ON AN EMPTY STOMACH.
PERMISSION TO SCREAM IN SHEER TERROR, SIR?
WOW! THE SECRET BASE REALLY IS BIG WHEN YOU GET UP CLOSE, ISN'T IT?

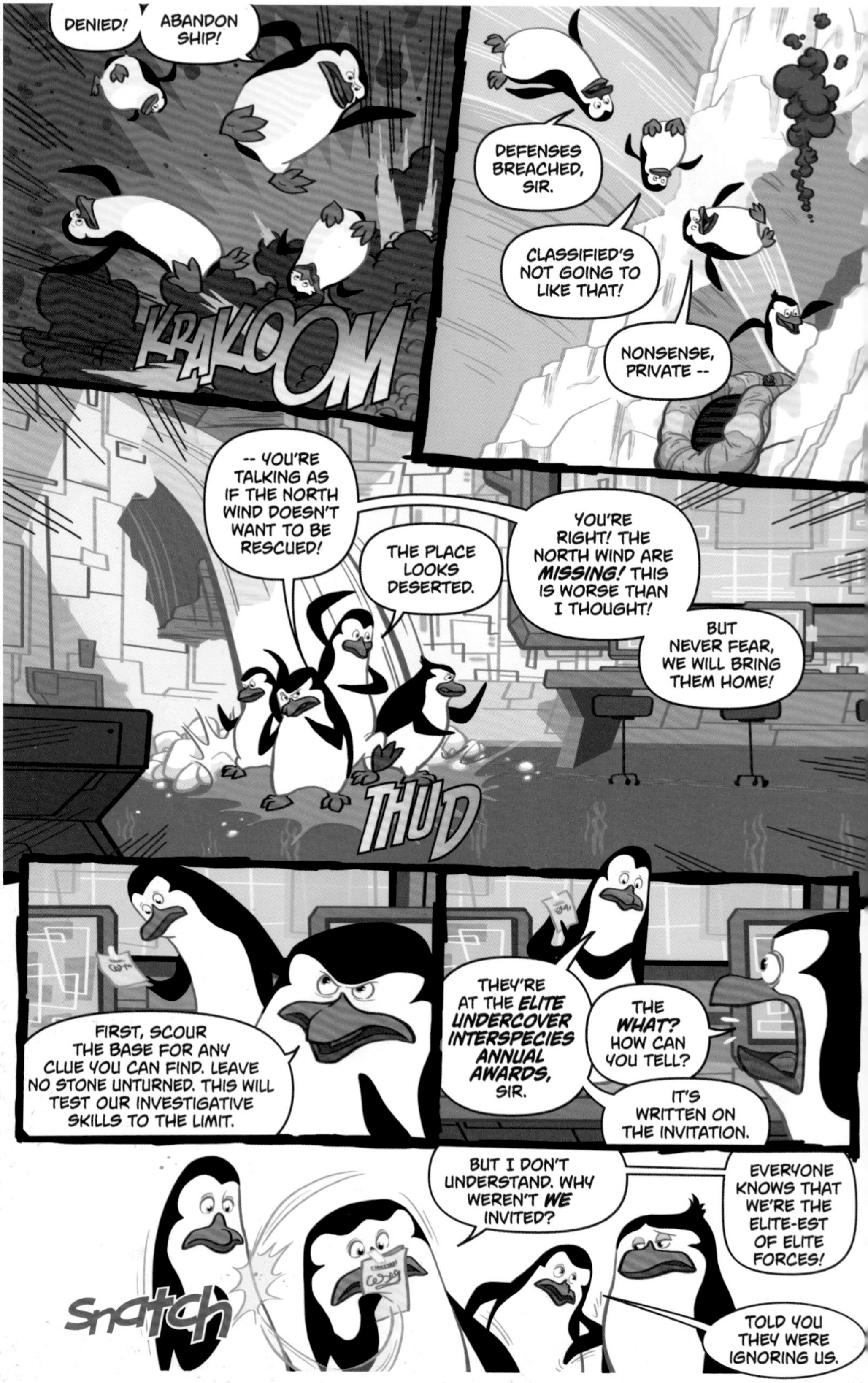
DENIED!
ABANDON SHIP!
KRAKOOM
DEFENSES BREACHED, SIR.
CLASSIFIED'S NOT GOING TO LIKE THAT!
NONSENSE, PRIVATE --
-- YOU'RE TALKING AS IF THE NORTH WIND DOESN'T WANT TO BE RESCUED!
THE PLACE LOOKS DESERTED.
YOU'RE RIGHT! THE NORTH WIND ARE MISSING! THIS IS WORSE THAN I THOUGHT!
BUT NEVER FEAR, WE WILL BRING THEM HOME!
THUD
FIRST, SCOUR THE BASE FOR ANY CLUE YOU CAN FIND. LEAVE NO STONE UNTURNED. THIS WILL TEST OUR INVESTIGATIVE SKILLS TO THE LIMIT.
THEY'RE AT THE ELITE UNDERCOVER INTERSPECIES ANNUAL AWARDS, SIR.
THE WHAT? HOW CAN YOU TELL?
IT'S WRITTEN ON THE INVITATION.
SNATCH
BUT I DON'T UNDERSTAND. WHY WEREN'T WE INVITED?
EVERYONE KNOWS THAT WE'RE THE ELITE-EST OF ELITE FORCES!
TOLD YOU THEY WERE IGNORING US.

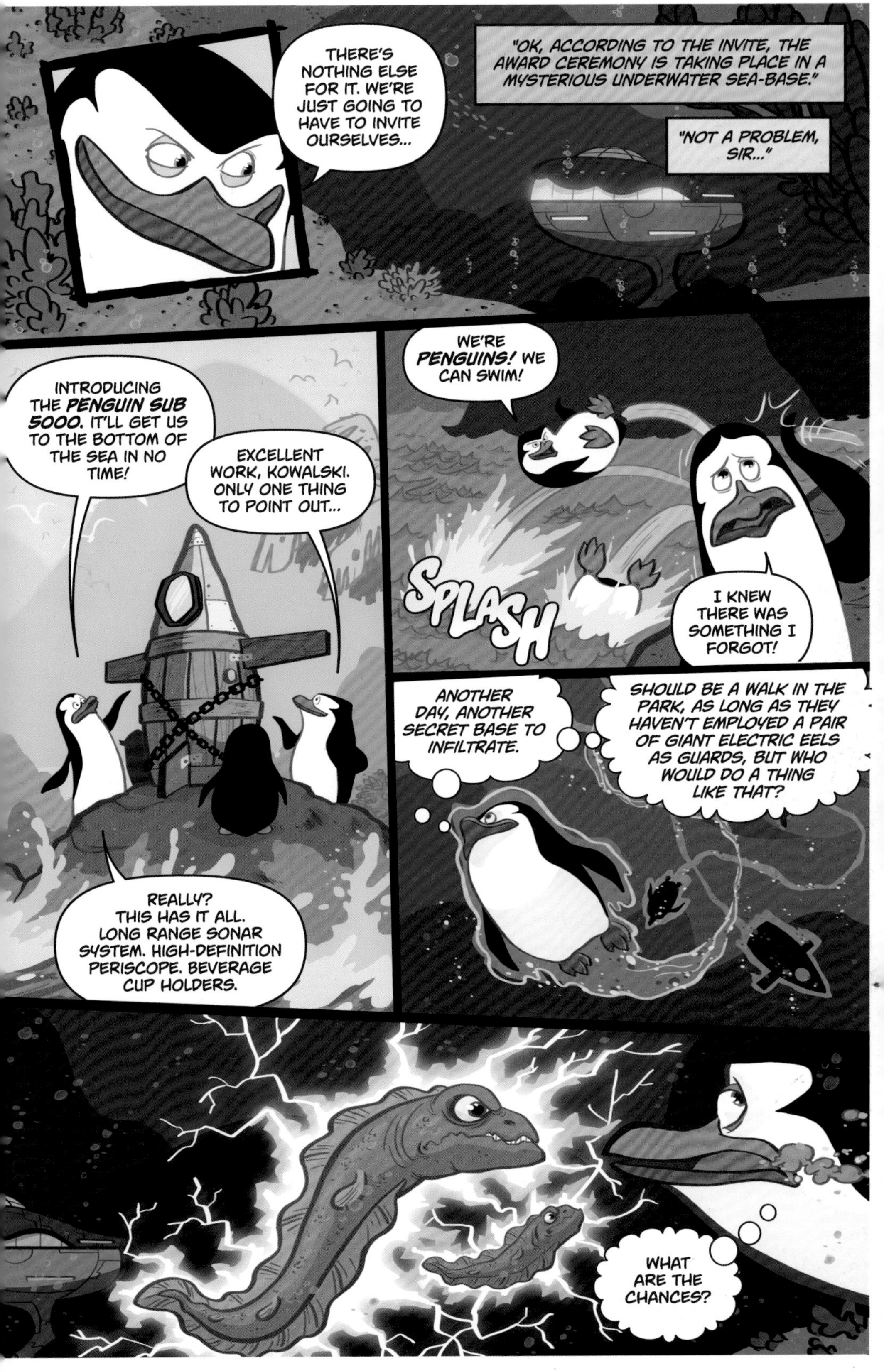
THERE'S NOTHING ELSE FOR IT. WE'RE JUST GOING TO HAVE TO INVITE OURSELVES...
"OK, ACCORDING TO THE INVITE, THE AWARD CEREMONY IS TAKING PLACE IN A MYSTERIOUS UNDERWATER SEA-BASE."
"NOT A PROBLEM, SIR..."
INTRODUCING THE PENGUIN SUB 5000. IT'LL GET US TO THE BOTTOM OF THE SEA IN NO TIME!
EXCELLENT WORK, KOWALSKI. ONLY ONE THING TO POINT OUT...
REALLY? THIS HAS IT ALL. LONG RANGE SONAR SYSTEM. HIGH-DEFINITION PERISCOPE. BEVERAGE CUP HOLDERS.
WE'RE PENGUINS! WE CAN SWIM!
SPLASH
I KNEW THERE WAS SOMETHING I FORGOT!
ANOTHER DAY, ANOTHER SECRET BASE TO INFILTRATE.
SHOULD BE A WALK IN THE PARK, AS LONG AS THEY HAVEN'T EMPLOYED A PAIR OF GIANT ELECTRIC EELS AS GUARDS, BUT WHO WOULD DO A THING LIKE THAT?
WHAT ARE THE CHANCES?

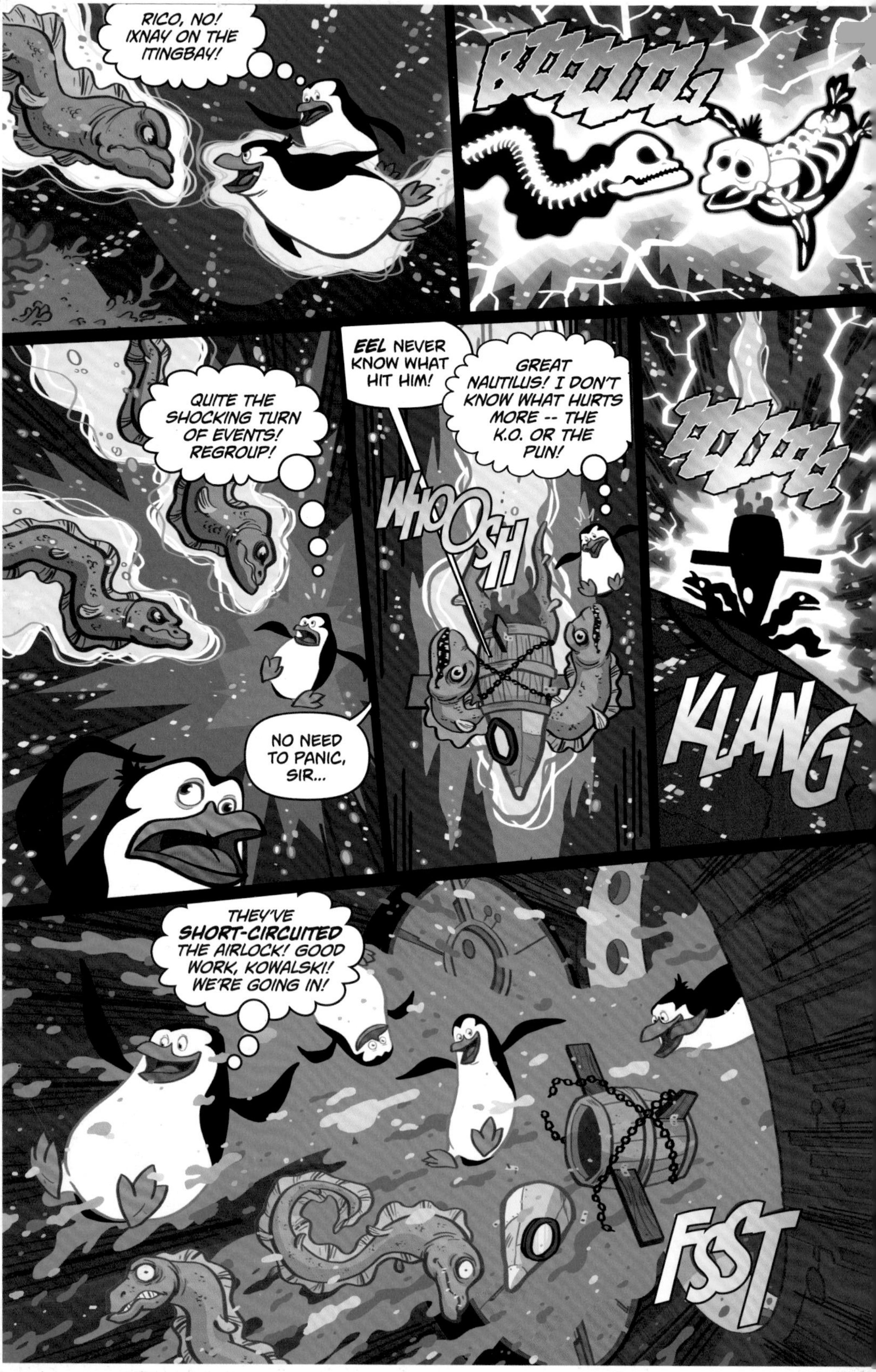
RICO, NO! IXNAY ON THE ITINGBAY!
QUITE THE SHOCKING TURN OF EVENTS! REGROUP!
NO NEED TO PANIC, SIR...
EEL NEVER KNOW WHAT HIT HIM!
GREAT NAUTILUS! I DON'T KNOW WHAT HURTS MORE -- THE K.O. OR THE PUN!
WHOOSH
KLANG
THEY'VE SHORT-CIRCUITED THE AIRLOCK! GOOD WORK, KOWALSKI! WE'RE GOING IN!
FSST

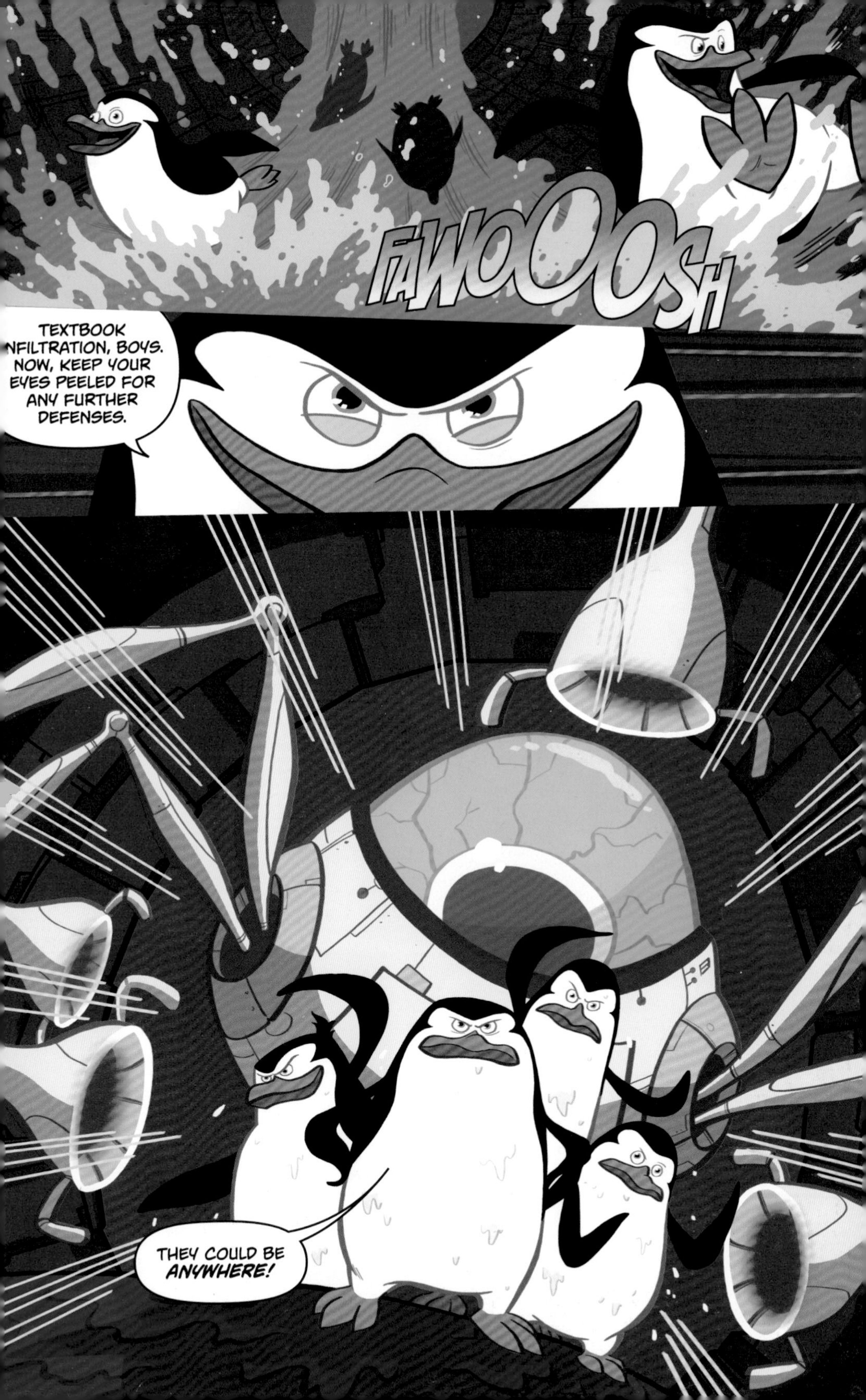
FAWOOOSH
TEXTBOOK NFILTRATION, BOYS. NOW, KEEP YOUR EYES PEELED FOR ANY FURTHER DEFENSES.
THEY COULD BE *ANYWHERE!*

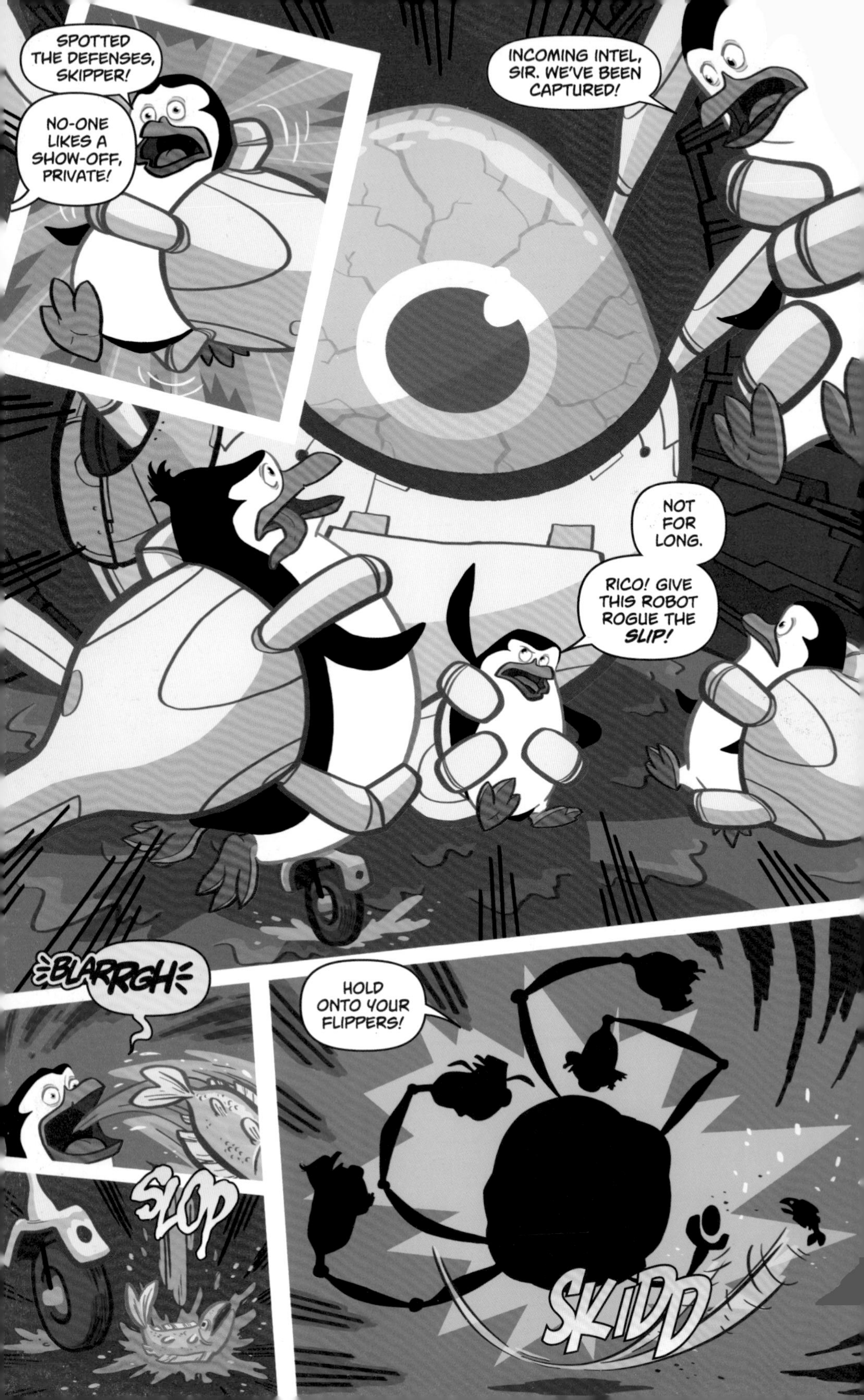
SPOTTED THE DEFENSES, SKIPPER!
NO-ONE LIKES A SHOW-OFF, PRIVATE!
INCOMING INTEL, SIR. WE'VE BEEN CAPTURED!
NOT FOR LONG.
RICO! GIVE THIS ROBOT ROGUE THE SLIP!
BLARRGH
HOLD ONTO YOUR FLIPPERS!
SLOP
SKIDD

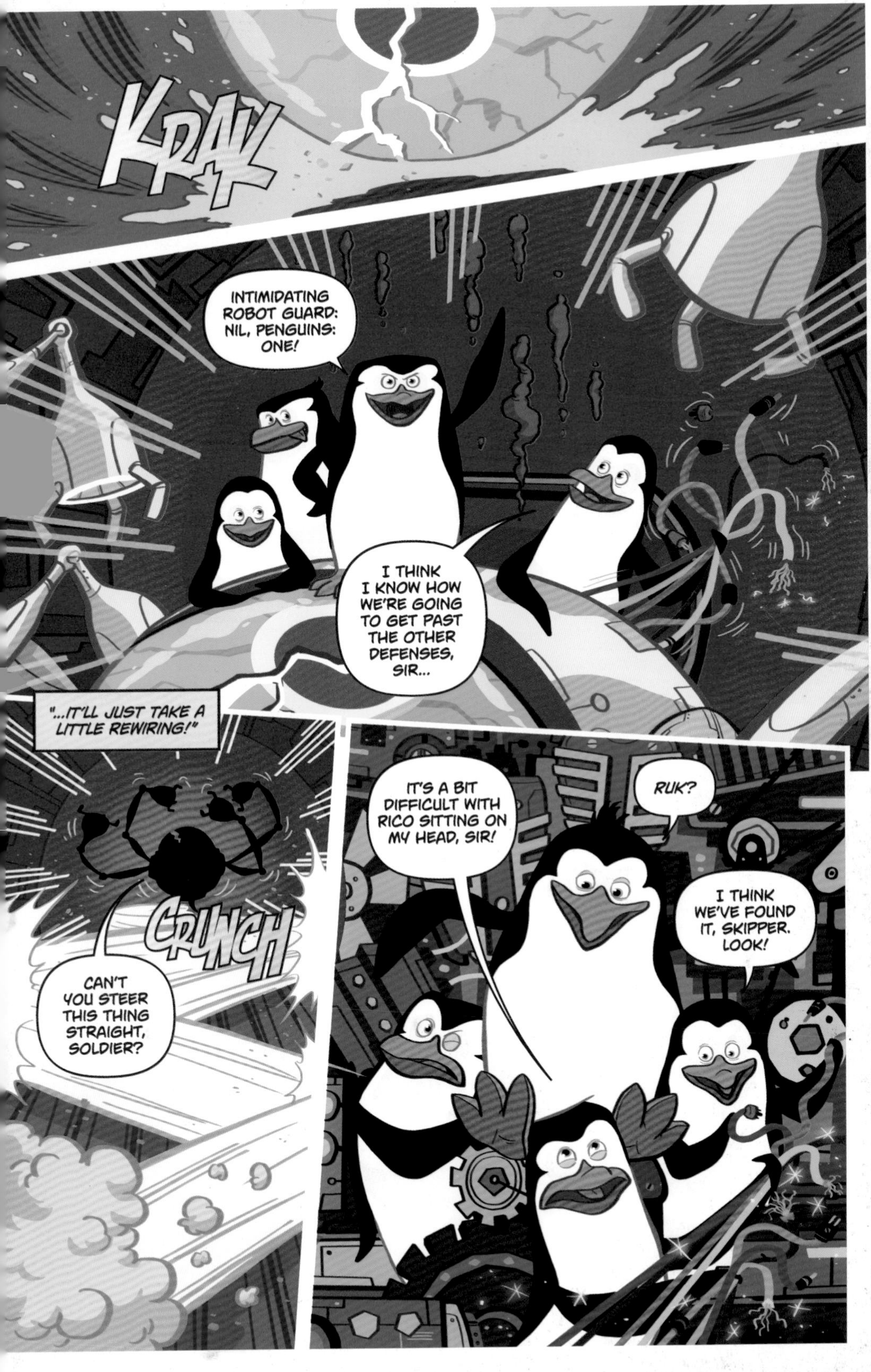
KRAK
INTIMIDATING ROBOT GUARD: NIL, PENGUINS: ONE!
I THINK I KNOW HOW WE'RE GOING TO GET PAST THE OTHER DEFENSES, SIR...
"...IT'LL JUST TAKE A LITTLE REWIRING!"
CRUNCH
CAN'T YOU STEER THIS THING STRAIGHT, SOLDIER?
IT'S A BIT DIFFICULT WITH RICO SITTING ON MY HEAD, SIR!
RUK?
I THINK WE'VE FOUND IT, SKIPPER. LOOK!

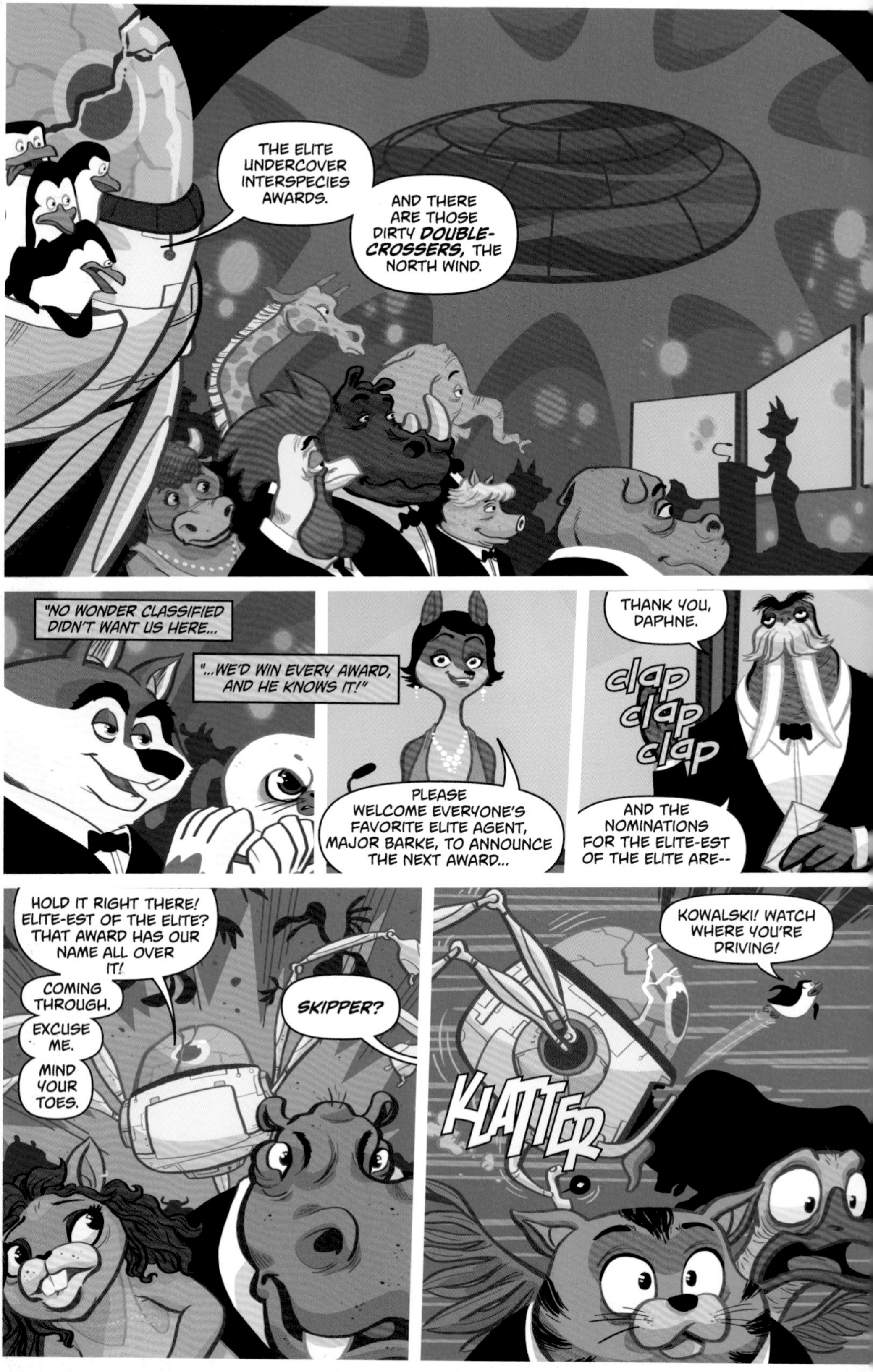
THE ELITE UNDERCOVER INTERSPECIES AWARDS.
AND THERE ARE THOSE DIRTY *DOUBLE-CROSSERS,* THE NORTH WIND.
"NO WONDER CLASSIFIED DIDN'T WANT US HERE...
"...WE'D WIN EVERY AWARD, AND HE KNOWS IT!"
PLEASE WELCOME EVERYONE'S FAVORITE ELITE AGENT, MAJOR BARKE, TO ANNOUNCE THE NEXT AWARD...
THANK YOU, DAPHNE.
clap clap clap
AND THE NOMINATIONS FOR THE ELITE-EST OF THE ELITE ARE--
HOLD IT RIGHT THERE! ELITE-EST OF THE ELITE? THAT AWARD HAS OUR NAME ALL OVER IT!
COMING THROUGH.
EXCUSE ME.
MIND YOUR TOES.
SKIPPER?
KOWALSKI! WATCH WHERE YOU'RE DRIVING!
KLATTER

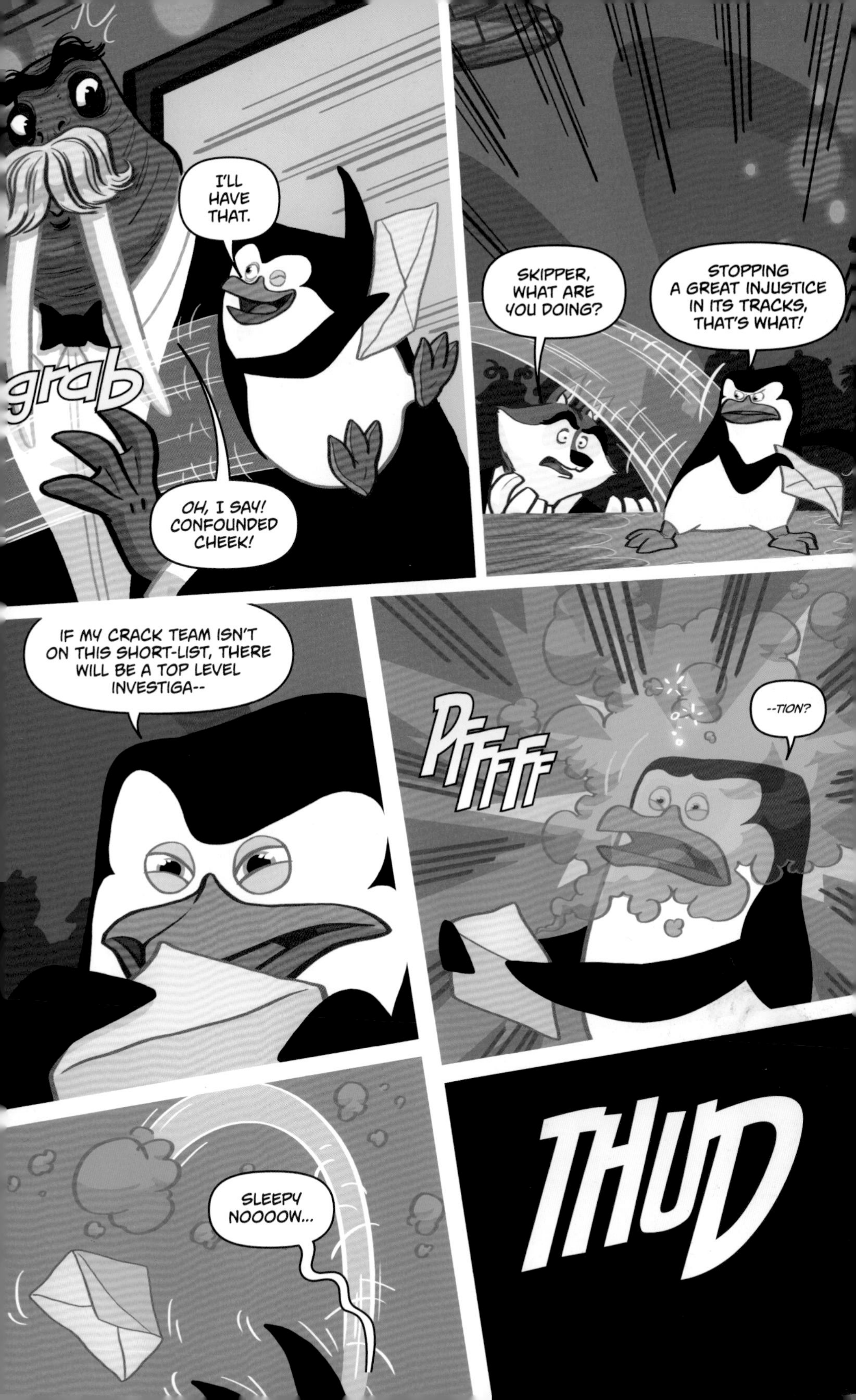
I'LL HAVE THAT.
grab
OH, I SAY! CONFOUNDED CHEEK!
SKIPPER, WHAT ARE YOU DOING?
STOPPING A GREAT INJUSTICE IN ITS TRACKS, THAT'S WHAT!
IF MY CRACK TEAM ISN'T ON THIS SHORT-LIST, THERE WILL BE A TOP LEVEL INVESTIGA--
PFFFFF
--TION?
SLEEPY NOOOOW...
THUD

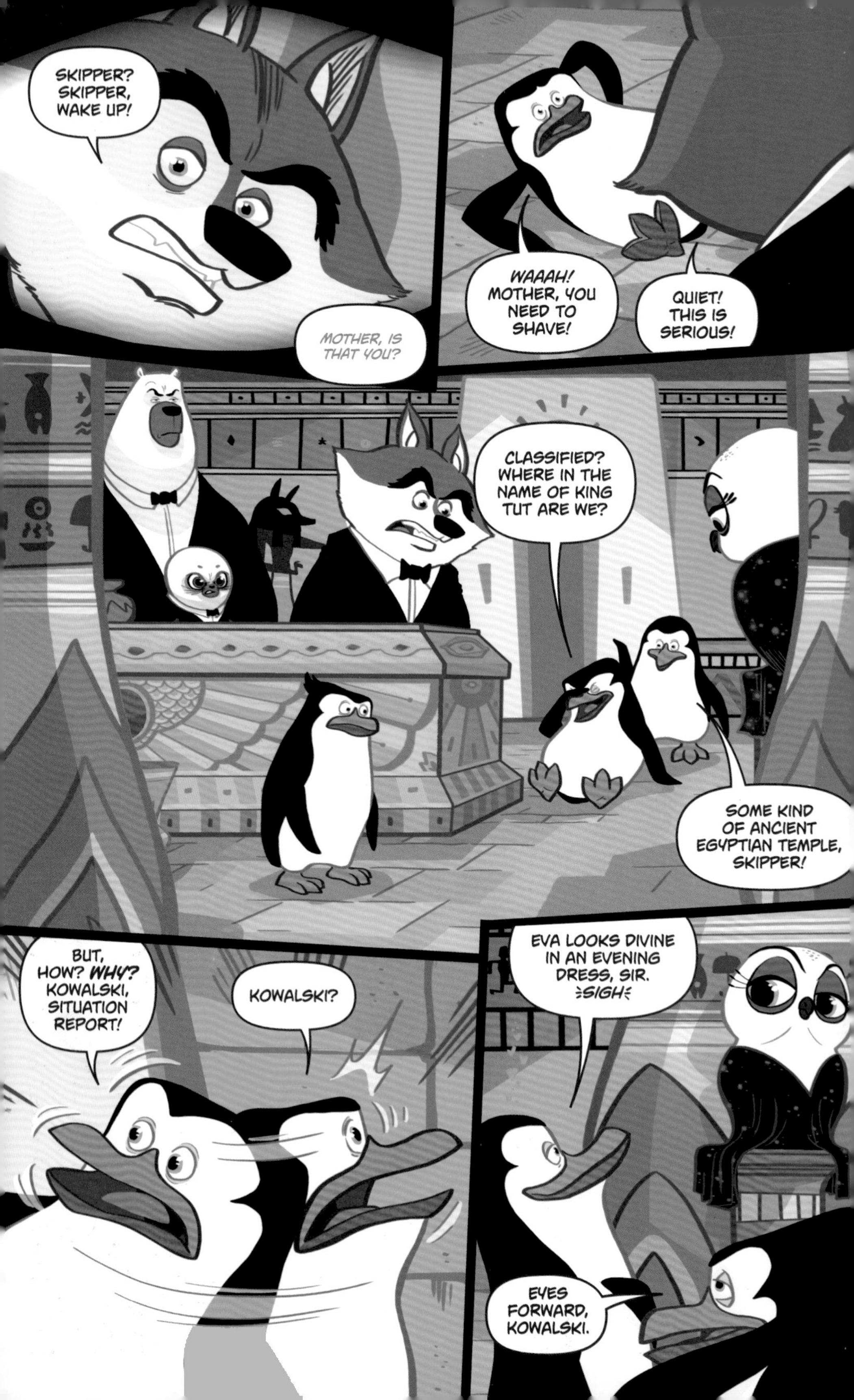
SKIPPER? SKIPPER, WAKE UP!
MOTHER, IS THAT YOU?
WAAAH! MOTHER, YOU NEED TO SHAVE!
QUIET! THIS IS SERIOUS!
CLASSIFIED? WHERE IN THE NAME OF KING TUT ARE WE?
SOME KIND OF ANCIENT EGYPTIAN TEMPLE, SKIPPER!
BUT, HOW? WHY? KOWALSKI, SITUATION REPORT!
KOWALSKI?
EVA LOOKS DIVINE IN AN EVENING DRESS, SIR. *SIGH*
EYES FORWARD, KOWALSKI.

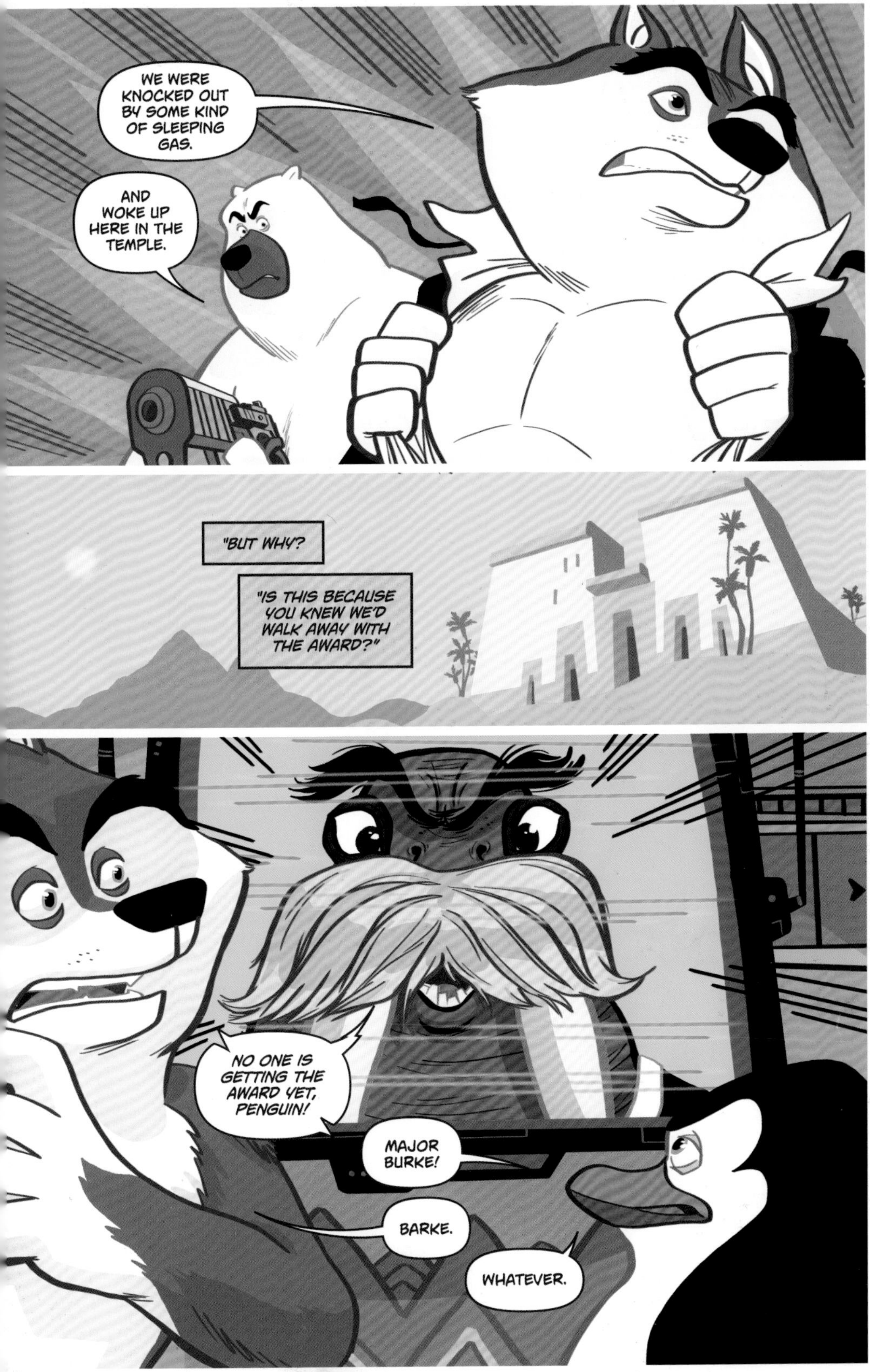
WE WERE KNOCKED OUT BY SOME KIND OF SLEEPING GAS.
AND WOKE UP HERE IN THE TEMPLE.
"BUT WHY?
"IS THIS BECAUSE YOU KNEW WE'D WALK AWAY WITH THE AWARD?"
NO ONE IS GETTING THE AWARD YET, PENGUIN!
MAJOR BURKE!
BARKE.
WHATEVER.

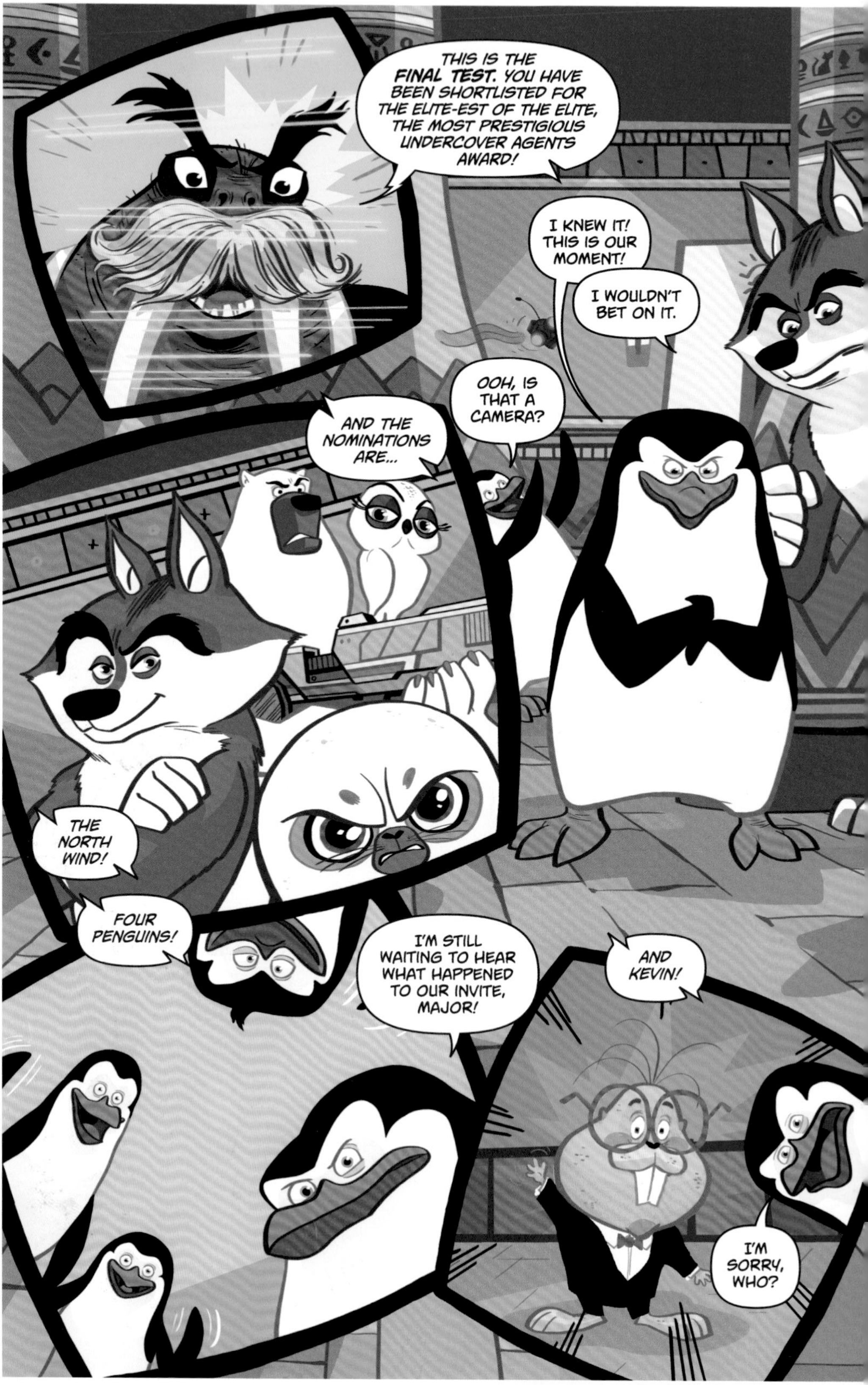
THIS IS THE FINAL TEST. YOU HAVE BEEN SHORTLISTED FOR THE ELITE-EST OF THE ELITE, THE MOST PRESTIGIOUS UNDERCOVER AGENTS AWARD!
I KNEW IT! THIS IS OUR MOMENT!
I WOULDN'T BET ON IT.
OOH, IS THAT A CAMERA?
AND THE NOMINATIONS ARE...
THE NORTH WIND!
FOUR PENGUINS!
I'M STILL WAITING TO HEAR WHAT HAPPENED TO OUR INVITE, MAJOR!
AND KEVIN!
I'M SORRY, WHO?

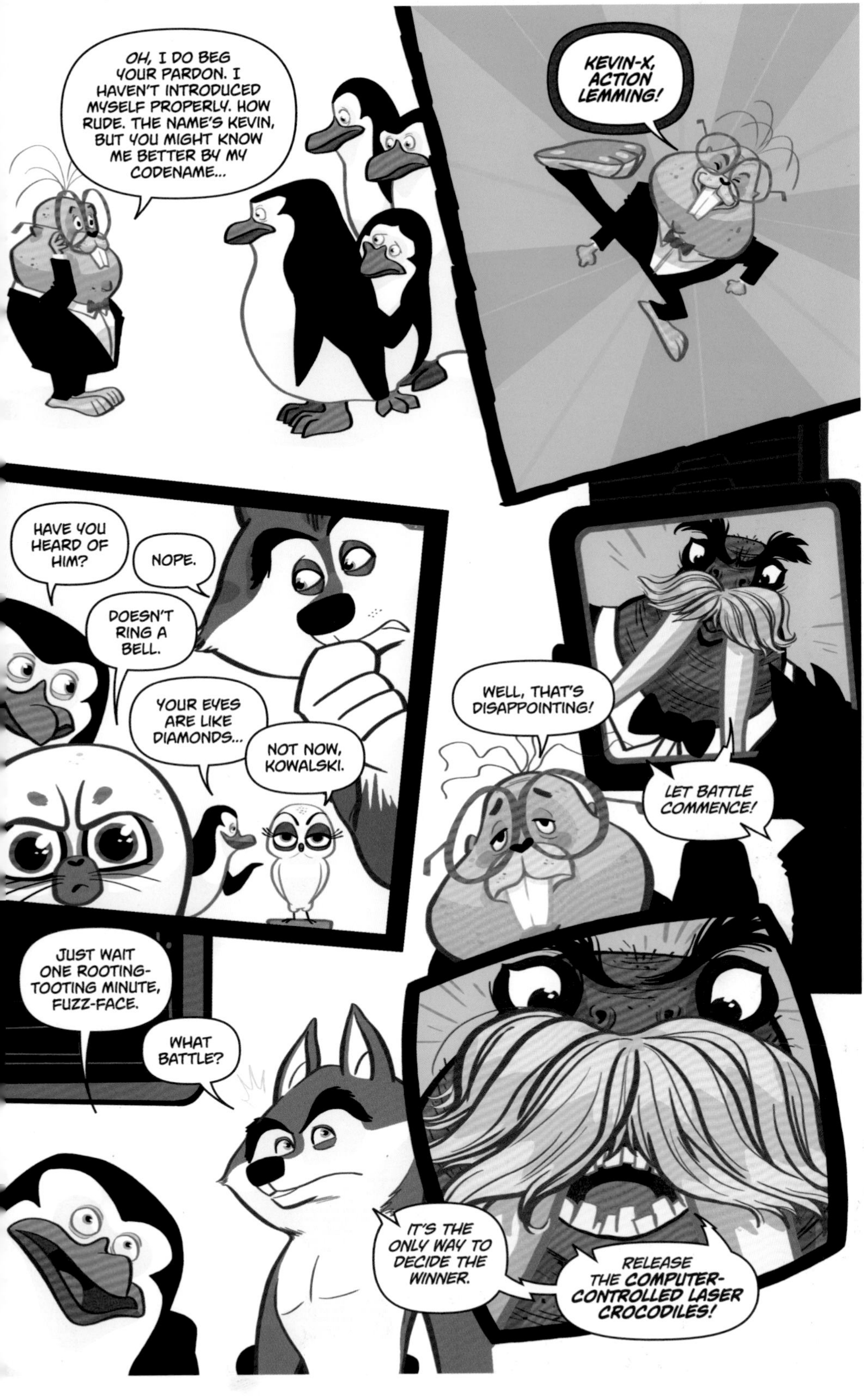
OH, I DO BEG YOUR PARDON. I HAVEN'T INTRODUCED MYSELF PROPERLY. HOW RUDE. THE NAME'S KEVIN, BUT YOU MIGHT KNOW ME BETTER BY MY CODENAME...
KEVIN-X, ACTION LEMMING!
HAVE YOU HEARD OF HIM?
NOPE.
DOESN'T RING A BELL.
YOUR EYES ARE LIKE DIAMONDS...
NOT NOW, KOWALSKI.
WELL, THAT'S DISAPPOINTING!
LET BATTLE COMMENCE!
JUST WAIT ONE ROOTING-TOOTING MINUTE, FUZZ-FACE.
WHAT BATTLE?
IT'S THE ONLY WAY TO DECIDE THE WINNER.
RELEASE THE COMPUTER-CONTROLLED LASER CROCODILES!

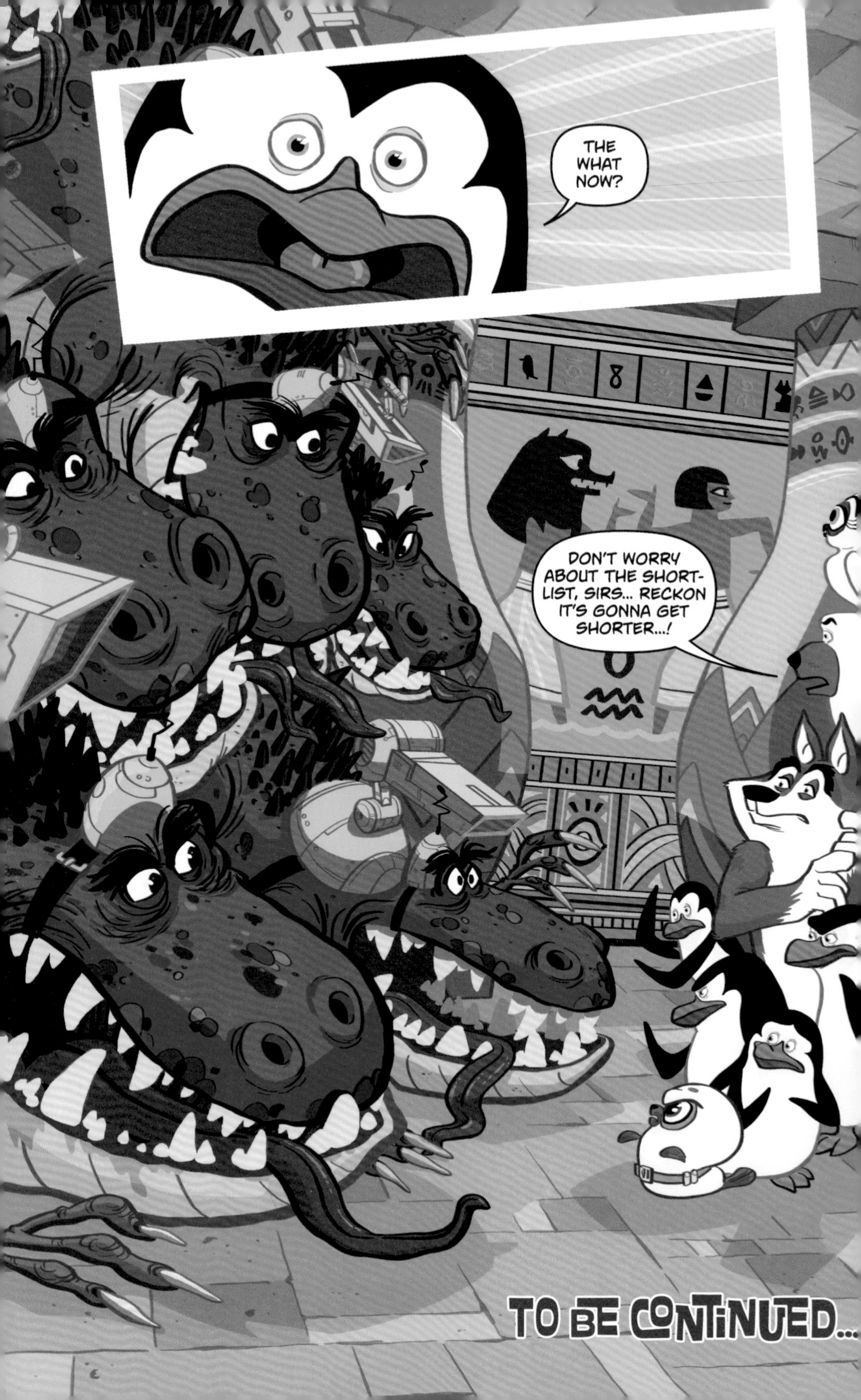
THE WHAT NOW?
DON'T WORRY ABOUT THE SHORT-LIST, SIRS... RECKON IT'S GONNA GET SHORTER...!
TO BE CONTINUED...

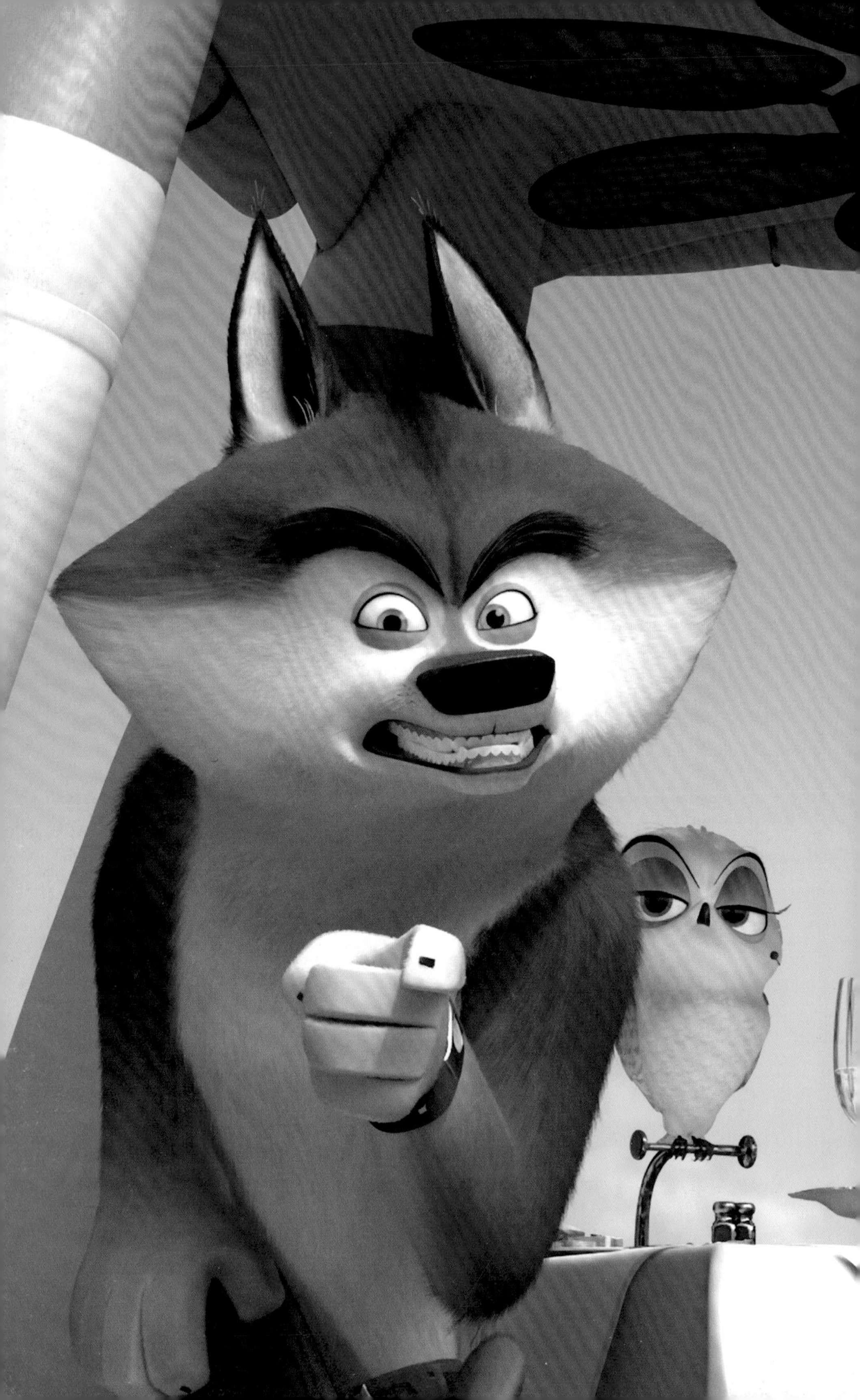

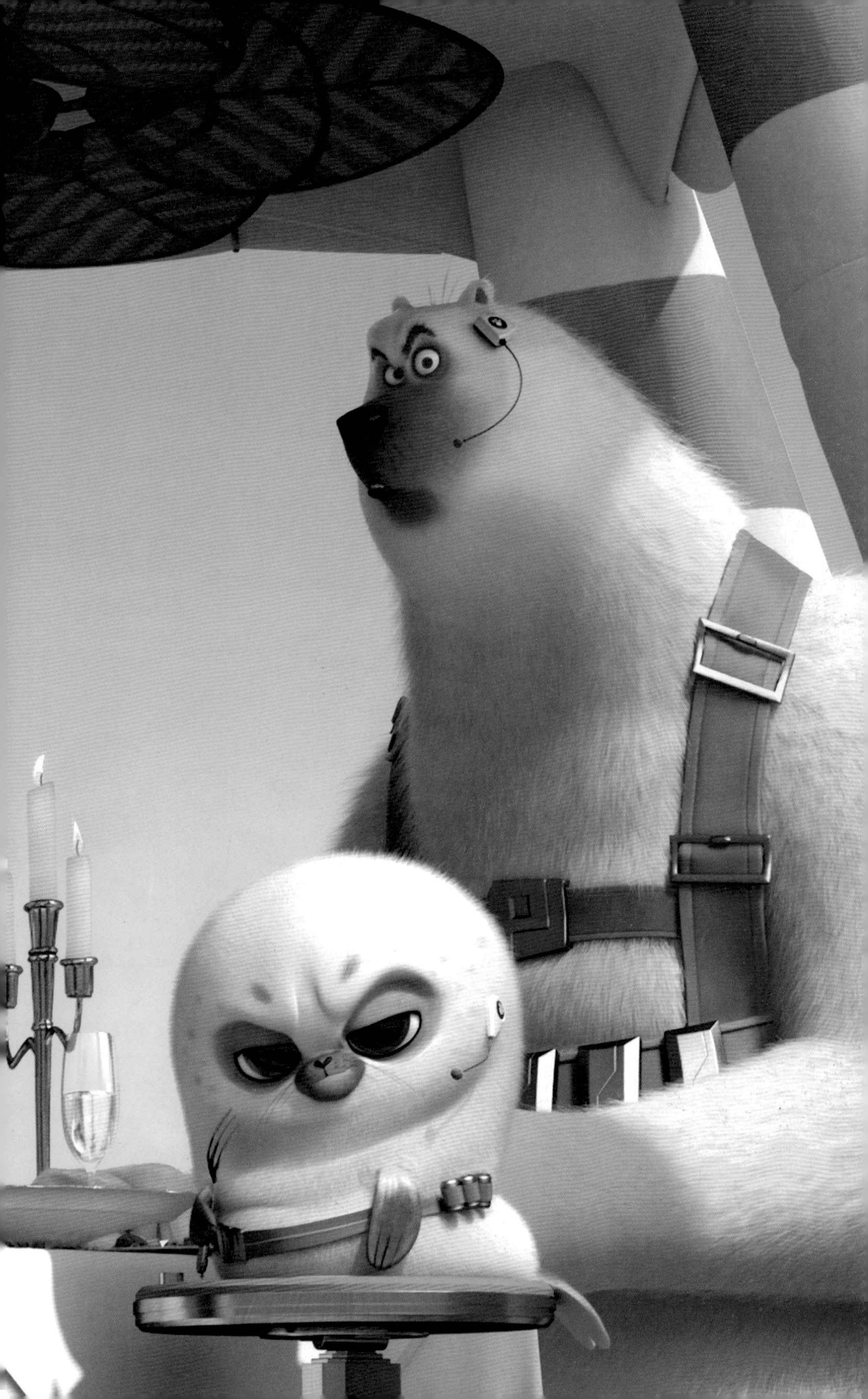

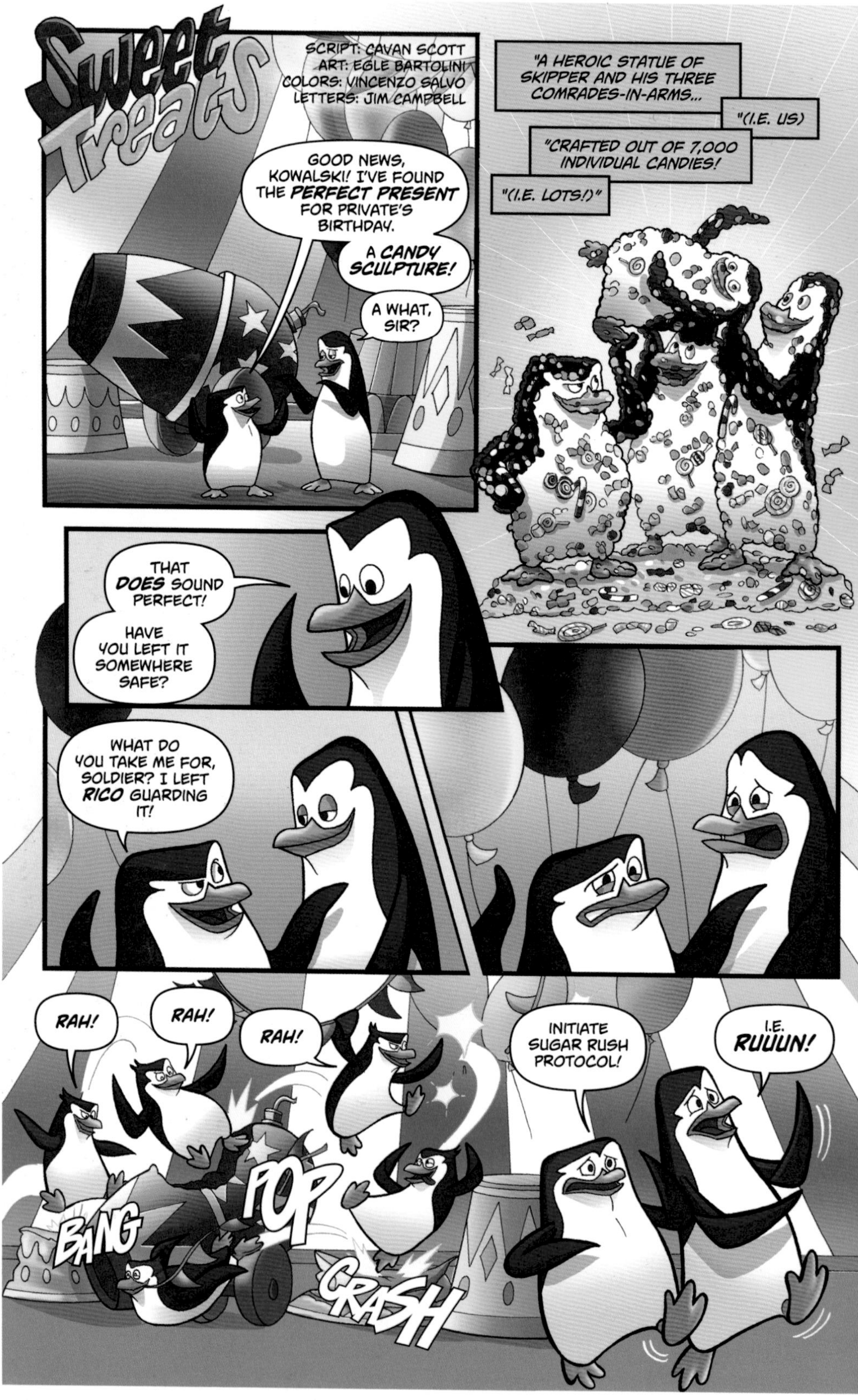
Sweet Treats
SCRIPT: CAVAN SCOTT
ART: EGLE BARTOLINI
COLORS: VINCENZO SALVO
LETTERS: JIM CAMPBELL
GOOD NEWS, KOWALSKI! I'VE FOUND THE PERFECT PRESENT FOR PRIVATE'S BIRTHDAY.
A CANDY SCULPTURE!
A WHAT, SIR?
"A HEROIC STATUE OF SKIPPER AND HIS THREE COMRADES-IN-ARMS...
"(I.E. US)
"CRAFTED OUT OF 7,000 INDIVIDUAL CANDIES!
"(I.E. LOTS!)"
THAT DOES SOUND PERFECT!
HAVE YOU LEFT IT SOMEWHERE SAFE?
WHAT DO YOU TAKE ME FOR, SOLDIER? I LEFT RICO GUARDING IT!
RAH!
RAH!
RAH!
BANG
POP
CRASH
INITIATE SUGAR RUSH PROTOCOL!
I.E. RUUUN!

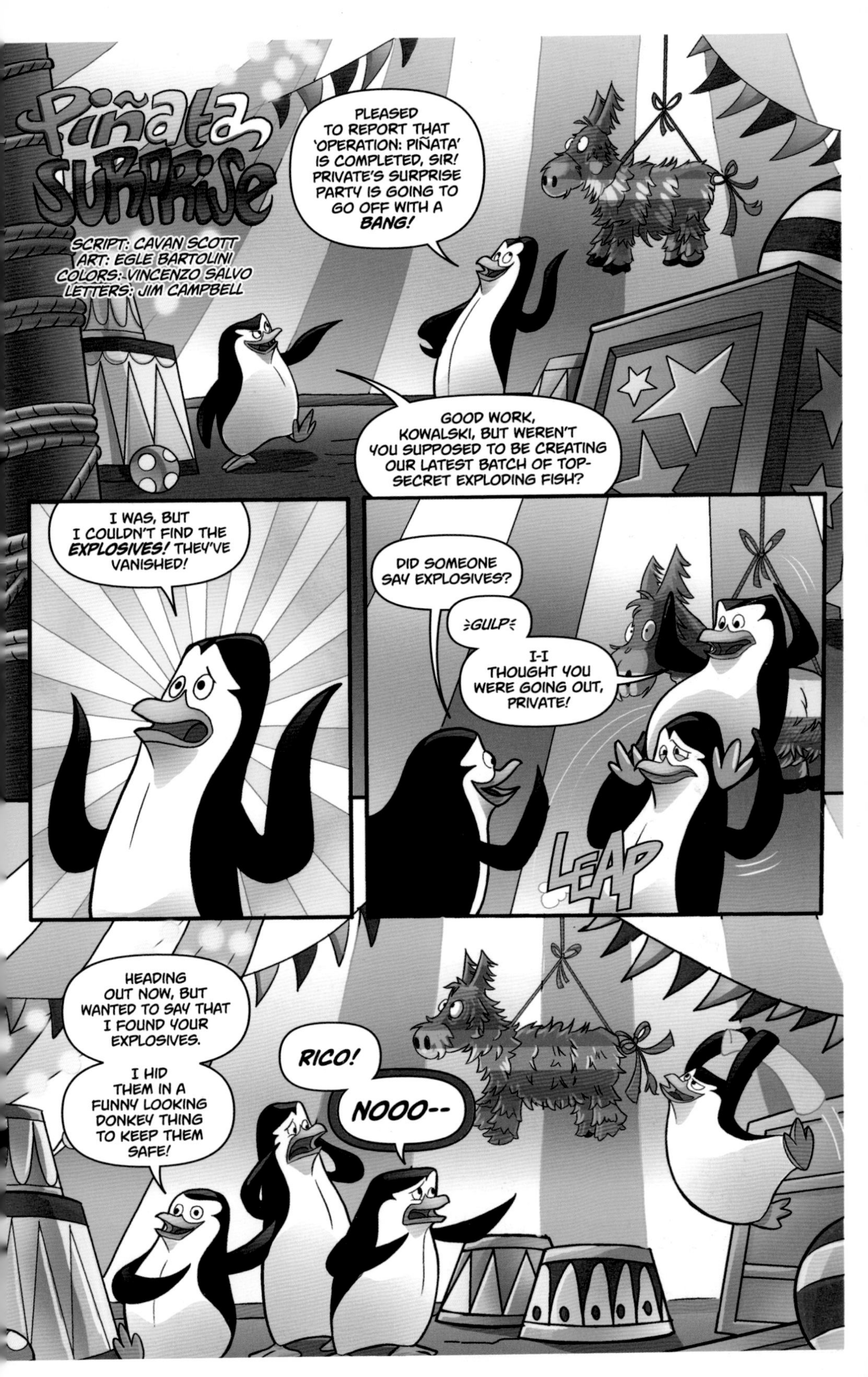
Piñata Surprise
SCRIPT: CAVAN SCOTT
ART: EGLE BARTOLINI
COLORS: VINCENZO SALVO
LETTERS: JIM CAMPBELL
PLEASED TO REPORT THAT 'OPERATION: PIÑATA' IS COMPLETED, SIR! PRIVATE'S SURPRISE PARTY IS GOING TO GO OFF WITH A BANG!
GOOD WORK, KOWALSKI, BUT WEREN'T YOU SUPPOSED TO BE CREATING OUR LATEST BATCH OF TOP-SECRET EXPLODING FISH?
I WAS, BUT I COULDN'T FIND THE EXPLOSIVES! THEY'VE VANISHED!
DID SOMEONE SAY EXPLOSIVES?
GULP
I-I THOUGHT YOU WERE GOING OUT, PRIVATE!
LEAP
HEADING OUT NOW, BUT WANTED TO SAY THAT I FOUND YOUR EXPLOSIVES.
I HID THEM IN A FUNNY LOOKING DONKEY THING TO KEEP THEM SAFE!
RICO!
NOOO--

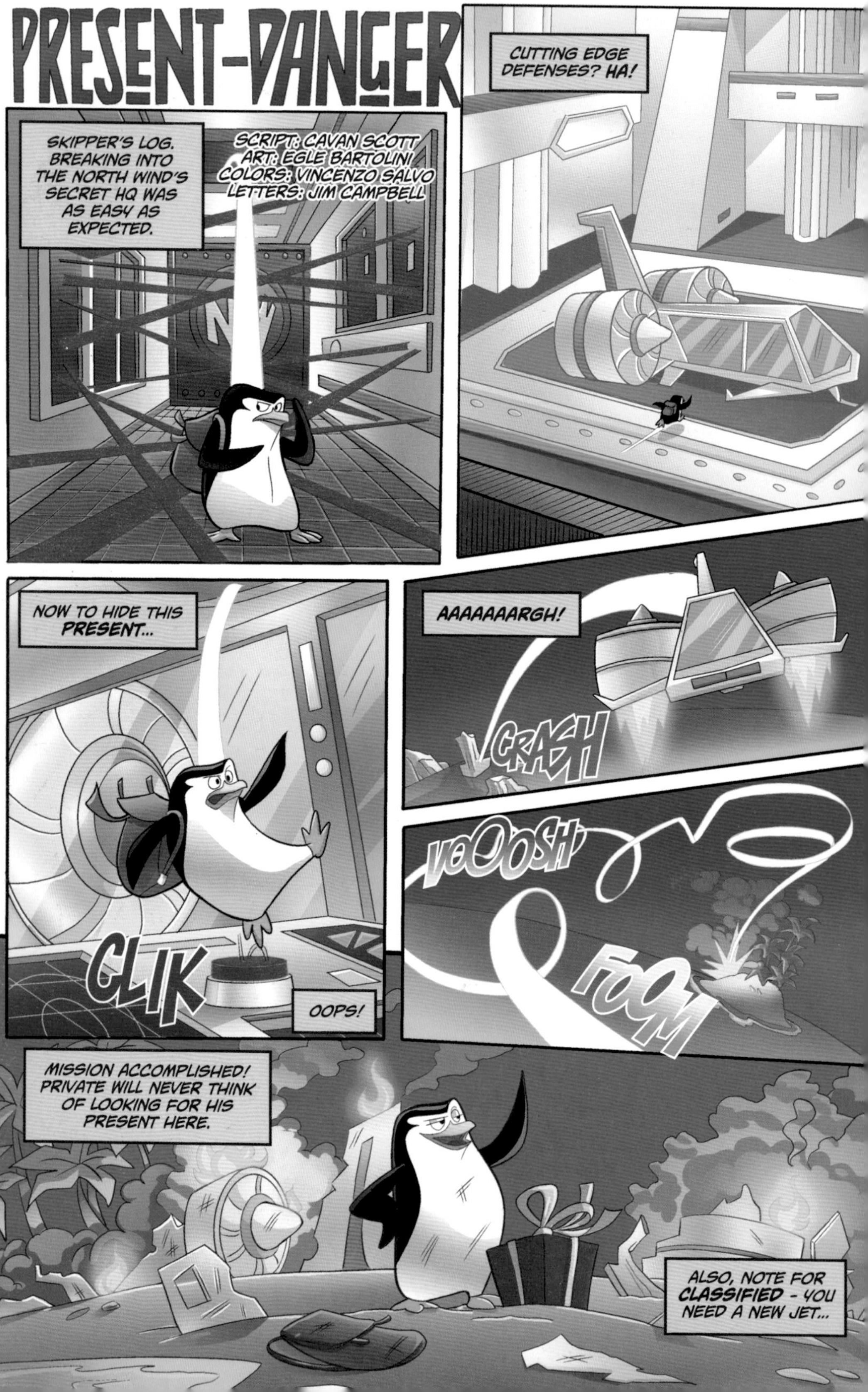
PRESENT-DANGER
SKIPPER'S LOG. BREAKING INTO THE NORTH WIND'S SECRET HQ WAS AS EASY AS EXPECTED.
SCRIPT: CAVAN SCOTT
ART: EGLE BARTOLINI
COLORS: VINCENZO SALVO
LETTERS: JIM CAMPBELL
CUTTING EDGE DEFENSES? HA!
NOW TO HIDE THIS PRESENT...
CLIK
OOPS!
AAAAAAARGH!
CRASH
VOOOOSH
FOOM
MISSION ACCOMPLISHED! PRIVATE WILL NEVER THINK OF LOOKING FOR HIS PRESENT HERE.
ALSO, NOTE FOR CLASSIFIED - YOU NEED A NEW JET...

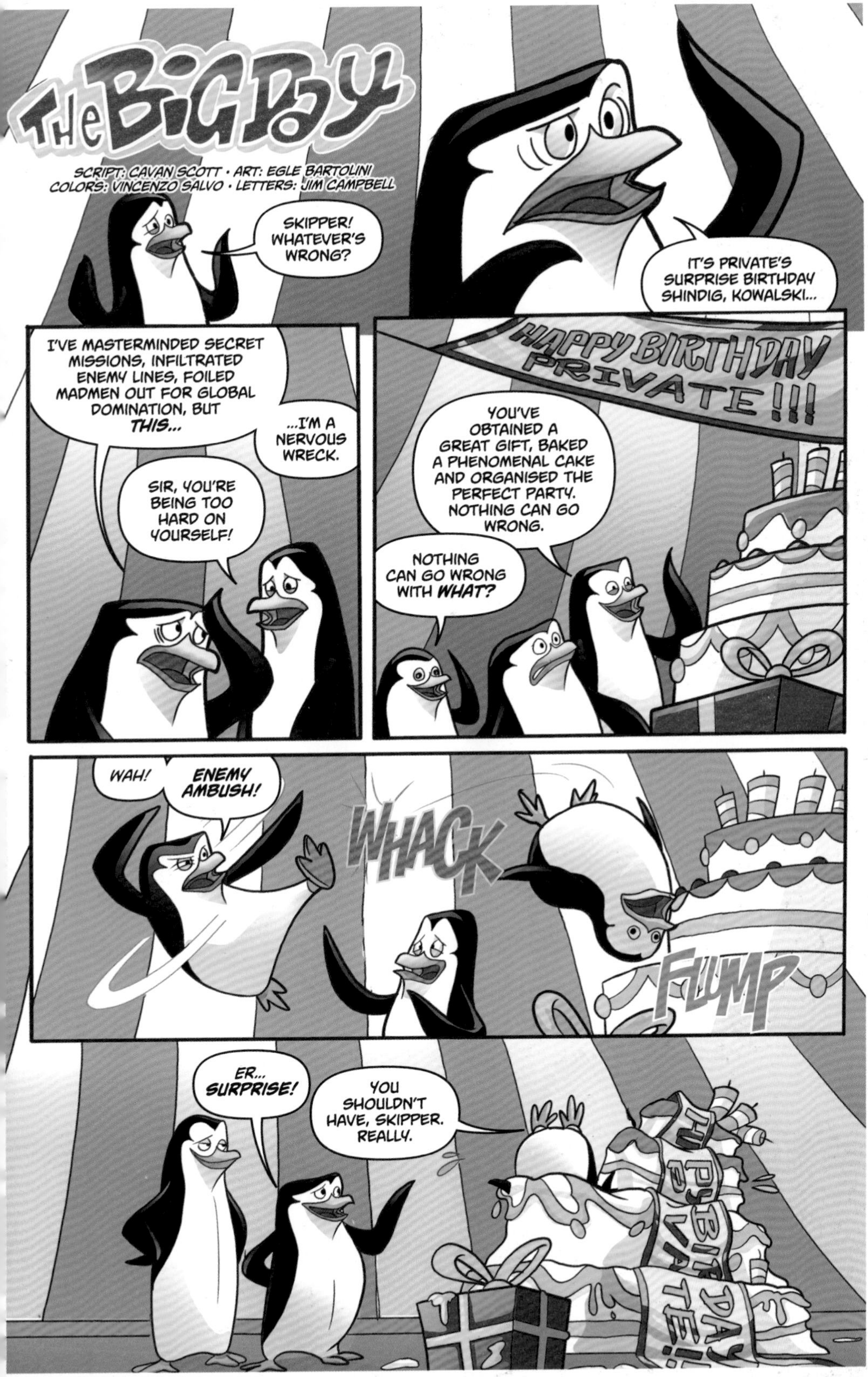
THE BIG DAY
SCRIPT: CAVAN SCOTT • ART: EGLE BARTOLINI
COLORS: VINCENZO SALVO • LETTERS: JIM CAMPBELL
SKIPPER! WHATEVER'S WRONG?
IT'S PRIVATE'S SURPRISE BIRTHDAY SHINDIG, KOWALSKI...
I'VE MASTERMINDED SECRET MISSIONS, INFILTRATED ENEMY LINES, FOILED MADMEN OUT FOR GLOBAL DOMINATION, BUT THIS...
...I'M A NERVOUS WRECK.
SIR, YOU'RE BEING TOO HARD ON YOURSELF!
HAPPY BIRTHDAY PRIVATE!!!
YOU'VE OBTAINED A GREAT GIFT, BAKED A PHENOMENAL CAKE AND ORGANISED THE PERFECT PARTY. NOTHING CAN GO WRONG.
NOTHING CAN GO WRONG WITH WHAT?
WAH!
ENEMY AMBUSH!
WHACK
FLUMP
ER... SURPRISE!
YOU SHOULDN'T HAVE, SKIPPER. REALLY.

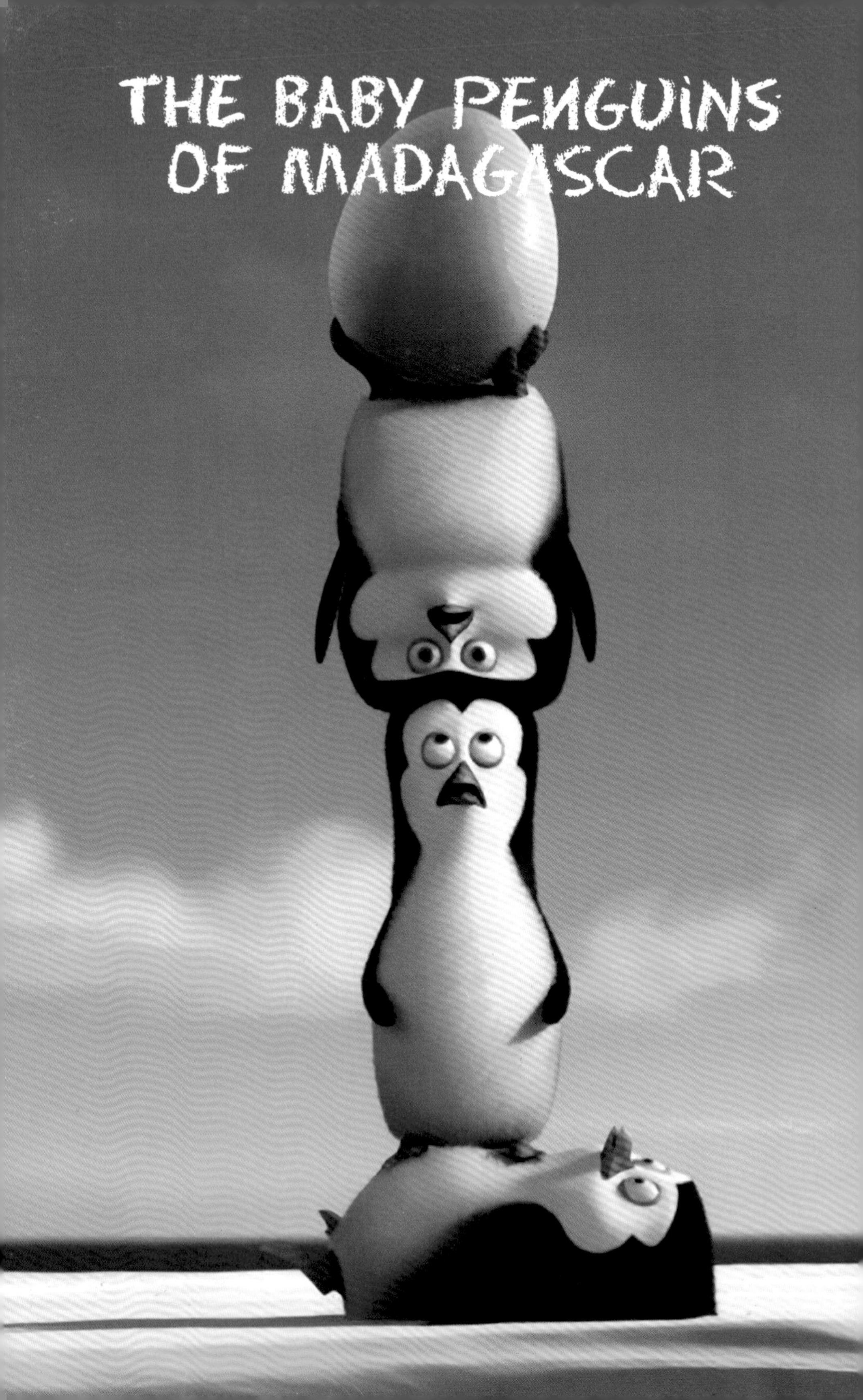
THE BABY PENGUINS
OF MADAGASCAR

THE BABY PENGUINS OF MADAGASCAR

ICE BABY PART 1

SCRIPT by Stuart Atholl GORDON • ART by Grant PERKINS • LETTERING by Jim CAMPBELL

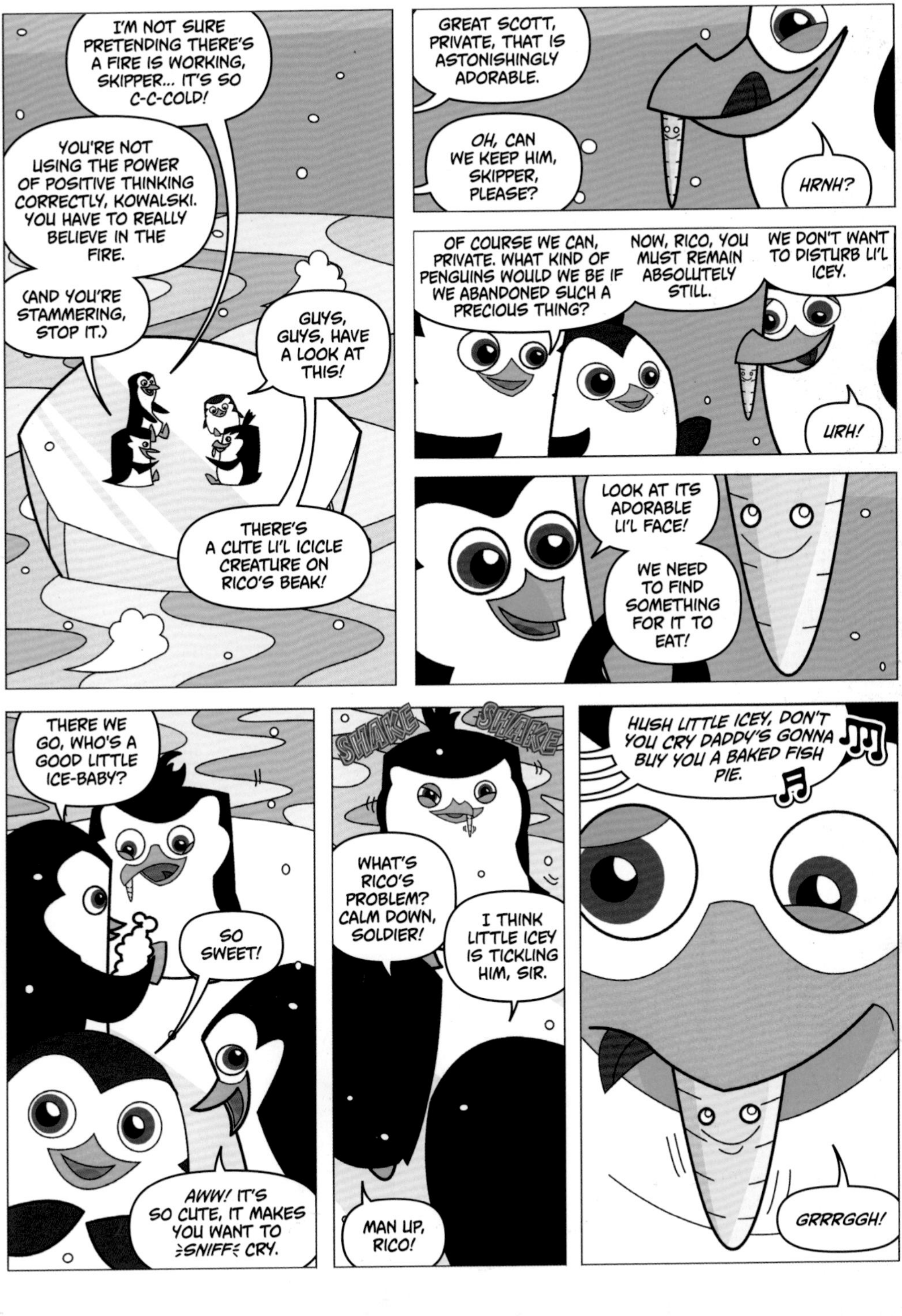

I'M NOT SURE PRETENDING THERE'S A FIRE IS WORKING, SKIPPER... IT'S SO C-C-COLD!
YOU'RE NOT USING THE POWER OF POSITIVE THINKING CORRECTLY, KOWALSKI. YOU HAVE TO REALLY BELIEVE IN THE FIRE.
(AND YOU'RE STAMMERING, STOP IT.)
GUYS, GUYS, HAVE A LOOK AT THIS!
THERE'S A CUTE LI'L ICICLE CREATURE ON RICO'S BEAK!
GREAT SCOTT, PRIVATE, THAT IS ASTONISHINGLY ADORABLE.
OH, CAN WE KEEP HIM, SKIPPER, PLEASE?
HRNH?
OF COURSE WE CAN, PRIVATE. WHAT KIND OF PENGUINS WOULD WE BE IF WE ABANDONED SUCH A PRECIOUS THING?
NOW, RICO, YOU MUST REMAIN ABSOLUTELY STILL.
WE DON'T WANT TO DISTURB LI'L ICEY.
URH!
LOOK AT ITS ADORABLE LI'L FACE!
WE NEED TO FIND SOMETHING FOR IT TO EAT!
THERE WE GO, WHO'S A GOOD LITTLE ICE-BABY?
SO SWEET!
AWW! IT'S SO CUTE, IT MAKES YOU WANT TO ≷SNIFF≶ CRY.
SHAKE
SHAKE
WHAT'S RICO'S PROBLEM? CALM DOWN, SOLDIER!
I THINK LITTLE ICEY IS TICKLING HIM, SIR.
MAN UP, RICO!
HUSH LITTLE ICEY, DON'T YOU CRY DADDY'S GONNA BUY YOU A BAKED FISH PIE.
GRRRGGH!

THE BABY PENGUINS OF MADAGASCAR

ICE BABY PART 2

SCRIPT by Stuart Atholl GORDON • ART by Grant PERKINS • LETTERING by Jim CAMPBELL

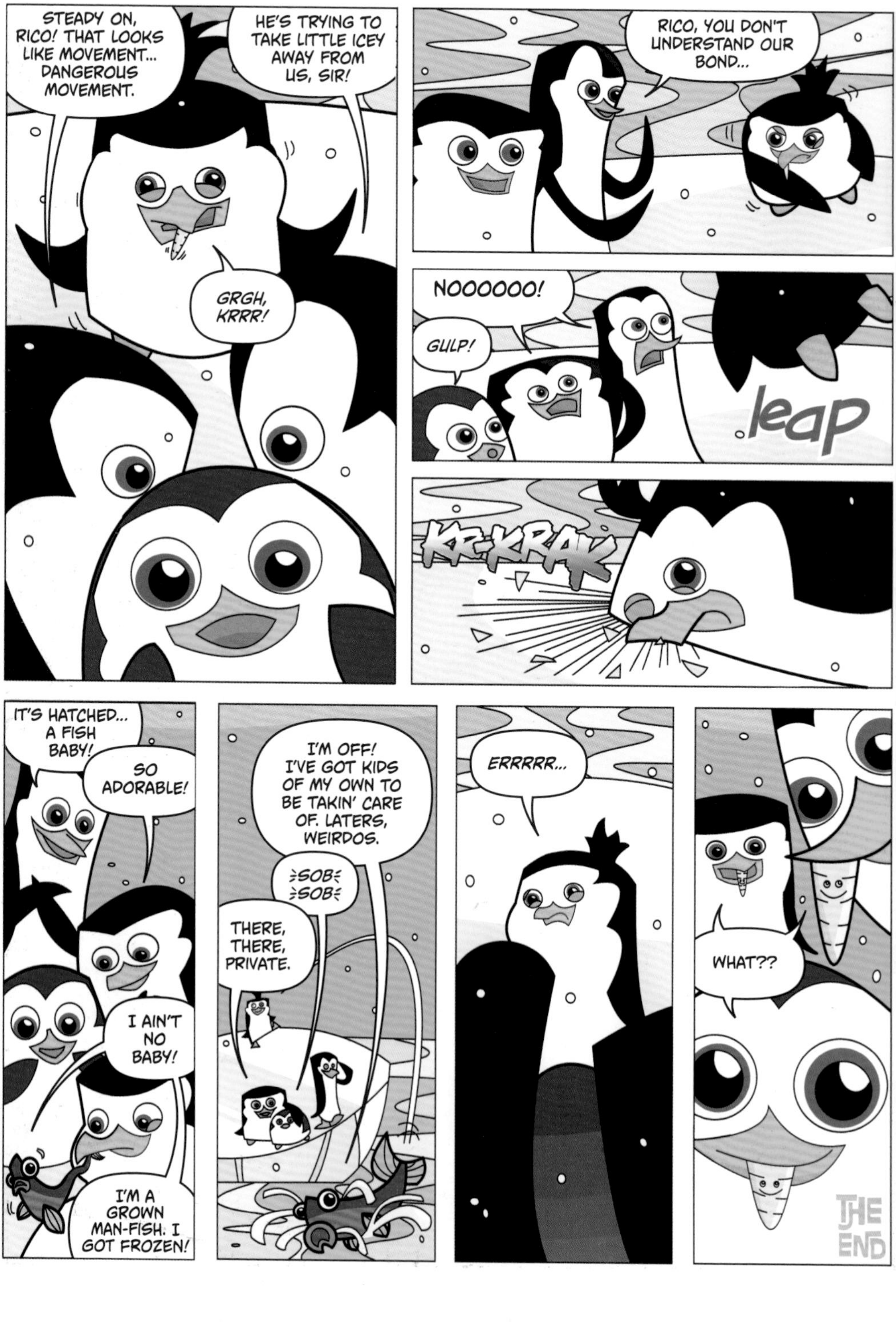

STEADY ON, RICO! THAT LOOKS LIKE MOVEMENT... DANGEROUS MOVEMENT.
HE'S TRYING TO TAKE LITTLE ICEY AWAY FROM US, SIR!
GRGH, KRRR!
RICO, YOU DON'T UNDERSTAND OUR BOND...
NOOOOOO!
GULP!
leap
KR-KRAK
IT'S HATCHED... A FISH BABY!
SO ADORABLE!
I AIN'T NO BABY!
I'M A GROWN MAN-FISH. I GOT FROZEN!
I'M OFF! I'VE GOT KIDS OF MY OWN TO BE TAKIN' CARE OF. LATERS, WEIRDOS.
SOB SOB
THERE, THERE, PRIVATE.
ERRRRR...
WHAT??
THE END

THE BABY PENGUINS OF MADAGASCAR
THE FROZEN TERROR! PART 1

SCRIPT by *Stuart Atholl GORDON* • ART by *Grant PERKINS* • LETTERING by *Jim CAMPBELL*

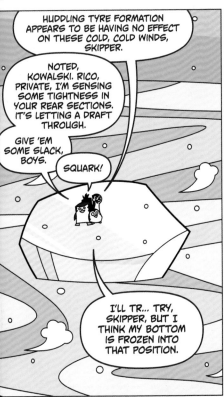

HUDDLING TYRE FORMATION APPEARS TO BE HAVING NO EFFECT ON THESE COLD, COLD WINDS, SKIPPER.

NOTED, KOWALSKI. RICO, PRIVATE, I'M SENSING SOME TIGHTNESS IN YOUR REAR SECTIONS. IT'S LETTING A DRAFT THROUGH.

GIVE 'EM SOME SLACK, BOYS.

SQUARK!

I'LL TR... TRY, SKIPPER, BUT I THINK MY BOTTOM IS FROZEN INTO THAT POSITION.

HUH! WHAT WAS THAT?

SKIPPER, DID YOU JUST SEE THAT... *SHADOWY SHAPE* OVER THERE?

I CAN'T SEE *ANYTHING* EXCEPT VAST FROZEN WASTES.

≷GASP≷ NOT SHADOWY, *HAIRY!*

UHH, GUYS, I THINK THERE IS A... *MONSTER* OUT THERE!

OH, SWEET, INNOCENT PRIVATE. THERE ARE NO SUCH THINGS AS MONSTERS.

THEY ONLY EXIST IN STORIES TO KEEP LITTLE PENGUINS IN AN ENDLESS LINE.

A *CLAW!* IT HAS A *HUMONGOUS HAIRY CLAW!*

JUST THE *ONE* CLAW, PRIVATE?

HEHEH!

MUST BE A REAL 'DRAG' CARRYING A SINGLE PINCHER AROUND.

BUT... BUT IT'S *OUT THERE!*

THE BABY PENGUINS OF MADAGASCAR

THE FROZEN TERROR! PART 2

SCRIPT by Stuart Atholl GORDON • ART by Grant PERKINS • LETTERING by Jim CAMPBELL

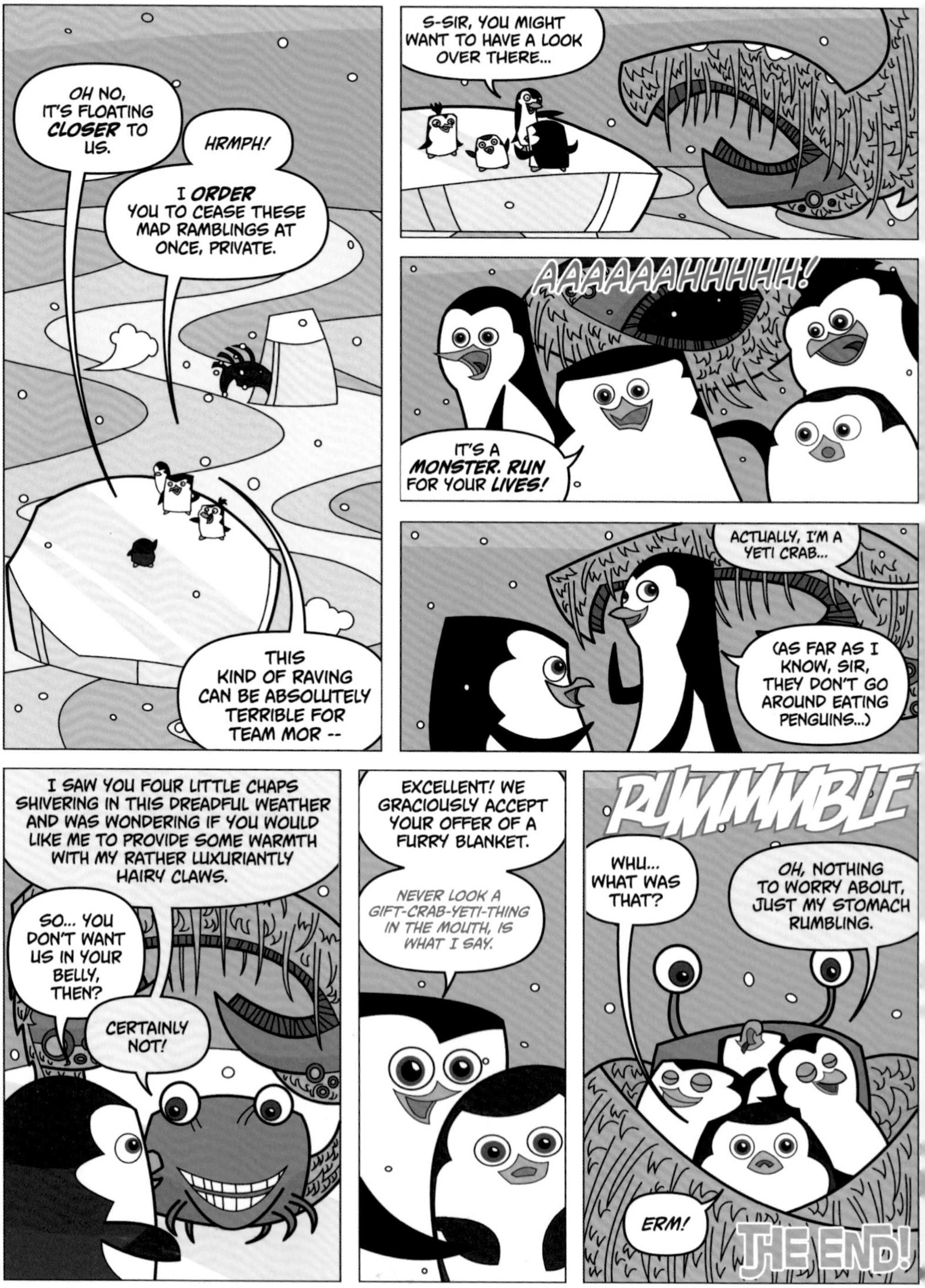
OH NO, IT'S FLOATING CLOSER TO US.
HRMPH!
I ORDER YOU TO CEASE THESE MAD RAMBLINGS AT ONCE, PRIVATE.
THIS KIND OF RAVING CAN BE ABSOLUTELY TERRIBLE FOR TEAM MOR --
S-SIR, YOU MIGHT WANT TO HAVE A LOOK OVER THERE...
AAAAAAAHHHHH!
IT'S A MONSTER. RUN FOR YOUR LIVES!
ACTUALLY, I'M A YETI CRAB...
(AS FAR AS I KNOW, SIR, THEY DON'T GO AROUND EATING PENGUINS...)
I SAW YOU FOUR LITTLE CHAPS SHIVERING IN THIS DREADFUL WEATHER AND WAS WONDERING IF YOU WOULD LIKE ME TO PROVIDE SOME WARMTH WITH MY RATHER LUXURIANTLY HAIRY CLAWS.
SO... YOU DON'T WANT US IN YOUR BELLY, THEN?
CERTAINLY NOT!
EXCELLENT! WE GRACIOUSLY ACCEPT YOUR OFFER OF A FURRY BLANKET.
NEVER LOOK A GIFT-CRAB-YETI-THING IN THE MOUTH, IS WHAT I SAY.
RUMMMBLE
WHU... WHAT WAS THAT?
OH, NOTHING TO WORRY ABOUT, JUST MY STOMACH RUMBLING.
ERM!
THE END!

COMING SOON

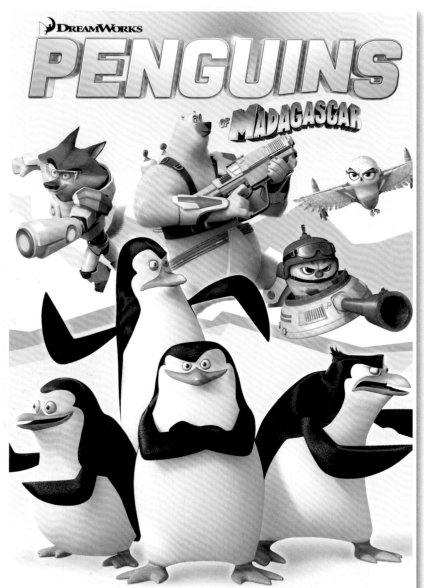

PENGUINS DIGEST FOUR!

WWW.TITAN-COMICS.COM
ALSO AVAILABLE DIGITALLY

TITAN COMICS GRAPHIC NOVELS

HOME: HOME SWEET HOME

PENGUINS OF MADAGASCAR:
THE GREAT DRAIN ROBBERY

KUNG FU PANDA –
READY, SET, PO!

DREAMWORKS DRAGONS:
RIDERS OF BERK – TALES FROM BERK

DREAMWORKS DRAGONS:
RIDERS OF BERK – THE ENEMIES WITHIN

DREAMWORKS DRAGONS: RIDERS OF BERK
COLLECTORS EDITION

DREAMWORKS DRAGONS:
MYTHS AND MYSTERIES
COMING SOON

WWW.TITAN-COMICS.COM

TITAN COMICS COMIC BOOKS

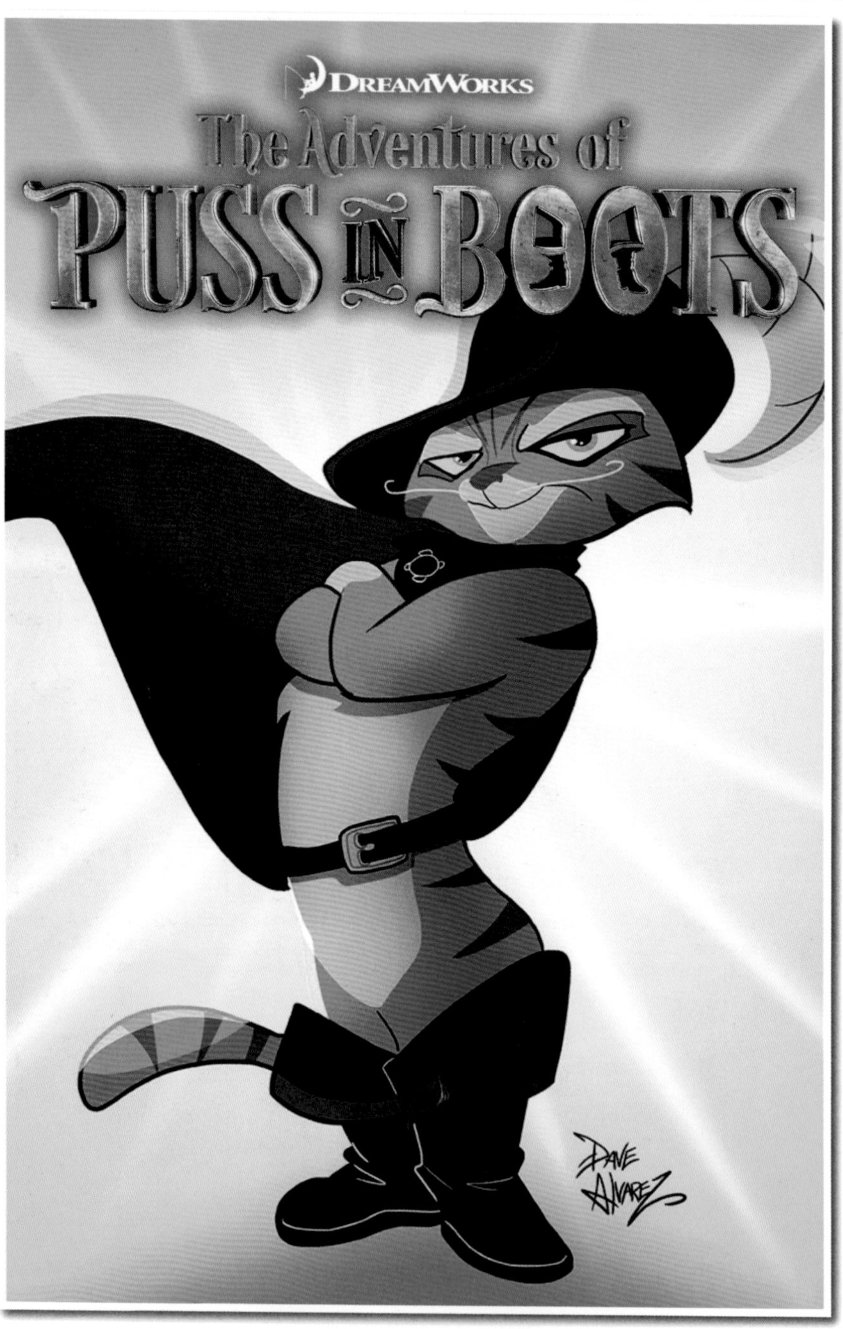
DreamWorks
The Adventures of
PUSS IN BOOTS
Dave Alvarez

AVAILABLE MONTHLY NOW!

ALSO AVAILABLE DIGITALLY.

WWW.TITAN-COMICS.COM

TITAN COMICS

DreamWorks Animation SKG

TITAN COMICS DIGESTS

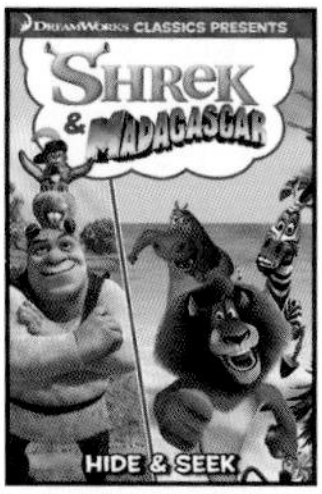
DreamWorks Classics Presents
Shrek & Madagascar
Hide & Seek

Dreamworks Classics – 'Hide & Seek'

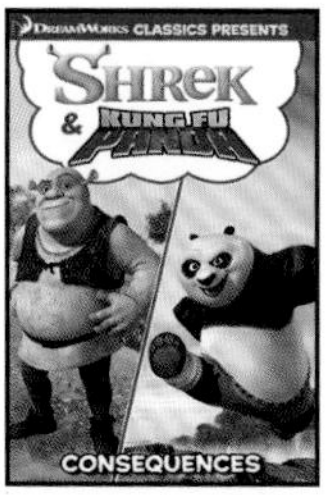
DreamWorks Classics Presents
Shrek & Kung Fu Panda
Consequences

Dreamworks Classics – 'Consequences'

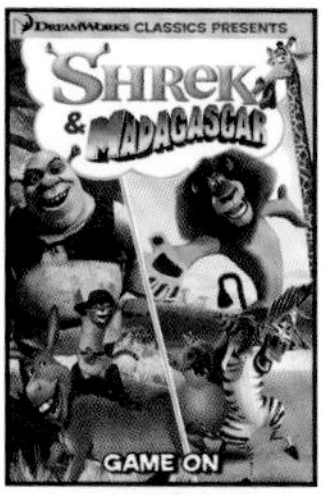
DreamWorks Classics Presents
Shrek & Madagascar
Game On

Dreamworks Classics – 'Game On'

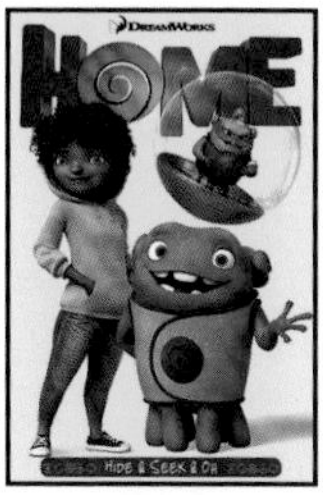
Home

Home – Hide & Seek & Oh

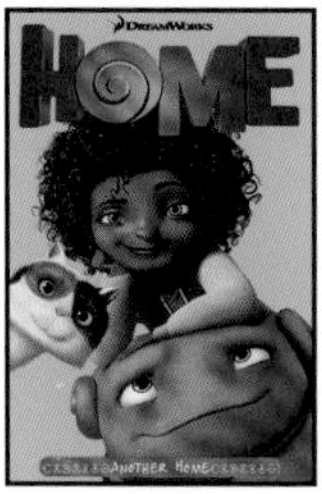
Home

Home – Another Home

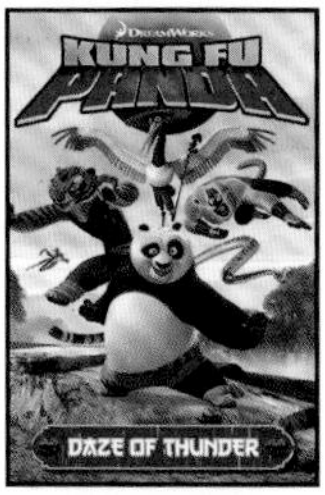
Kung Fu Panda
Daze of Thunder

Kung Fu Panda – Daze of Thunder

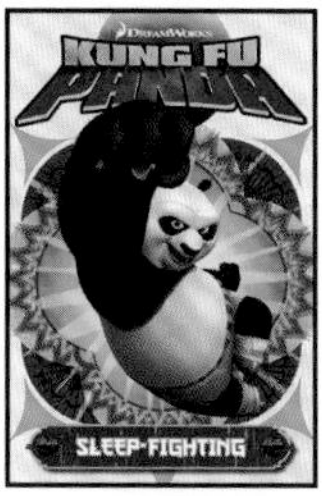
Kung Fu Panda
Sleep-Fighting

Kung Fu Panda – Sleep-Fighting

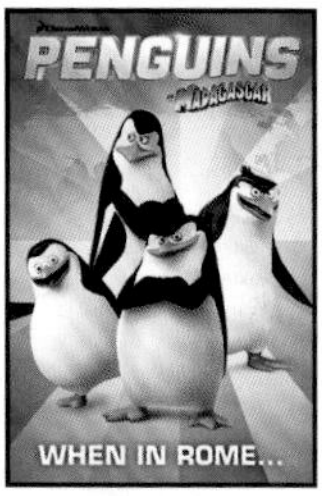
Penguins
When in Rome...

Penguins of Madagascar – When in Rome...

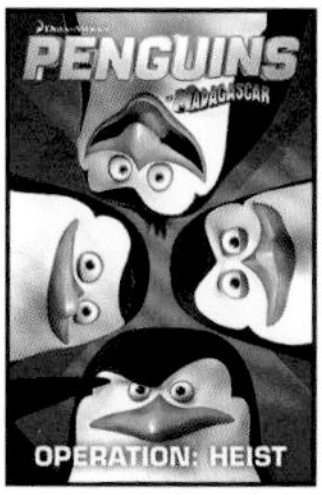
Penguins
Operation: Heist

Penguins of Madagascar – Operation: Heist

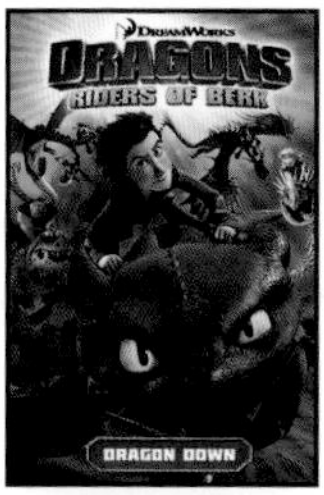
Dragons
Riders of Berk
Dragon Down

DreamWorks Dragons: Riders of Berk – Dragon Down

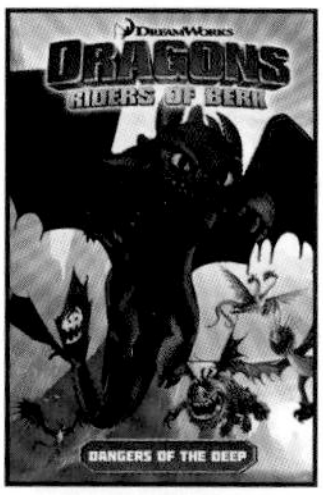
Dragons
Riders of Berk
Dangers of the Deep

DreamWorks Dragons: Riders of Berk – Dangers of the Deep

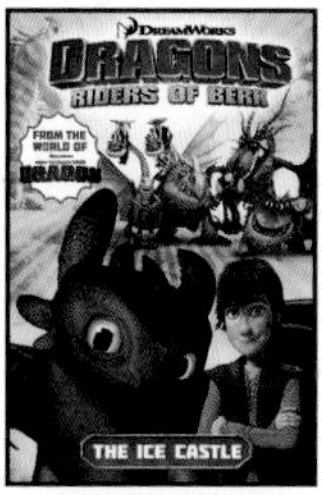
Dragons
Riders of Berk
The Ice Castle

DreamWorks Dragons: Riders of Berk – The Ice Castle

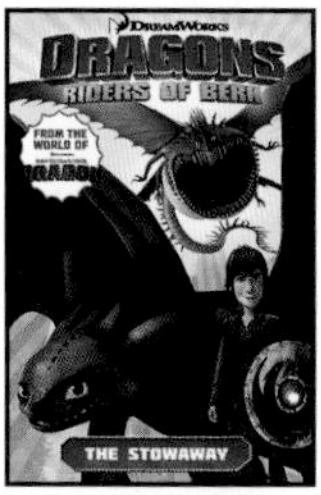
Dragons
Riders of Berk
The Stowaway

DreamWorks Dragons: Riders of Berk – The Stowaway

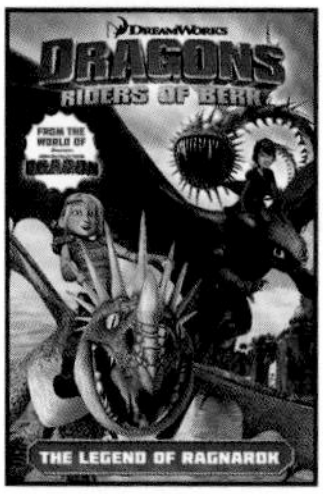
Dragons
Riders of Berk
The Legend of Ragnarok

DreamWorks Dragons: Riders of Berk – The Legend of Ragnarok

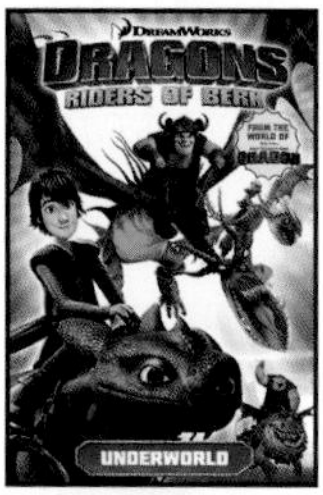
Dragons
Riders of Berk
Underworld

DreamWorks Dragons: Riders of Berk – Underworld

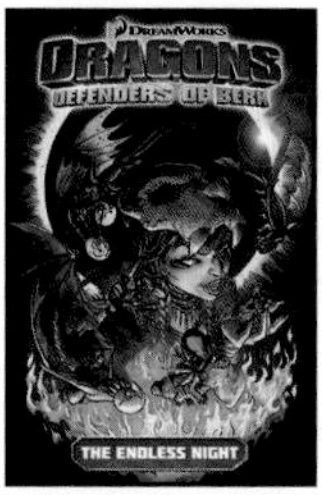
Dragons
Defenders of Berk
The Endless Night

DreamWorks Dragons: Defenders of Berk - The Endless Night

WWW.TITAN-COMICS.COM

ALSO AVAILABLE DIGITALLY

TITAN COMICS

DreamWorks Animation SKG

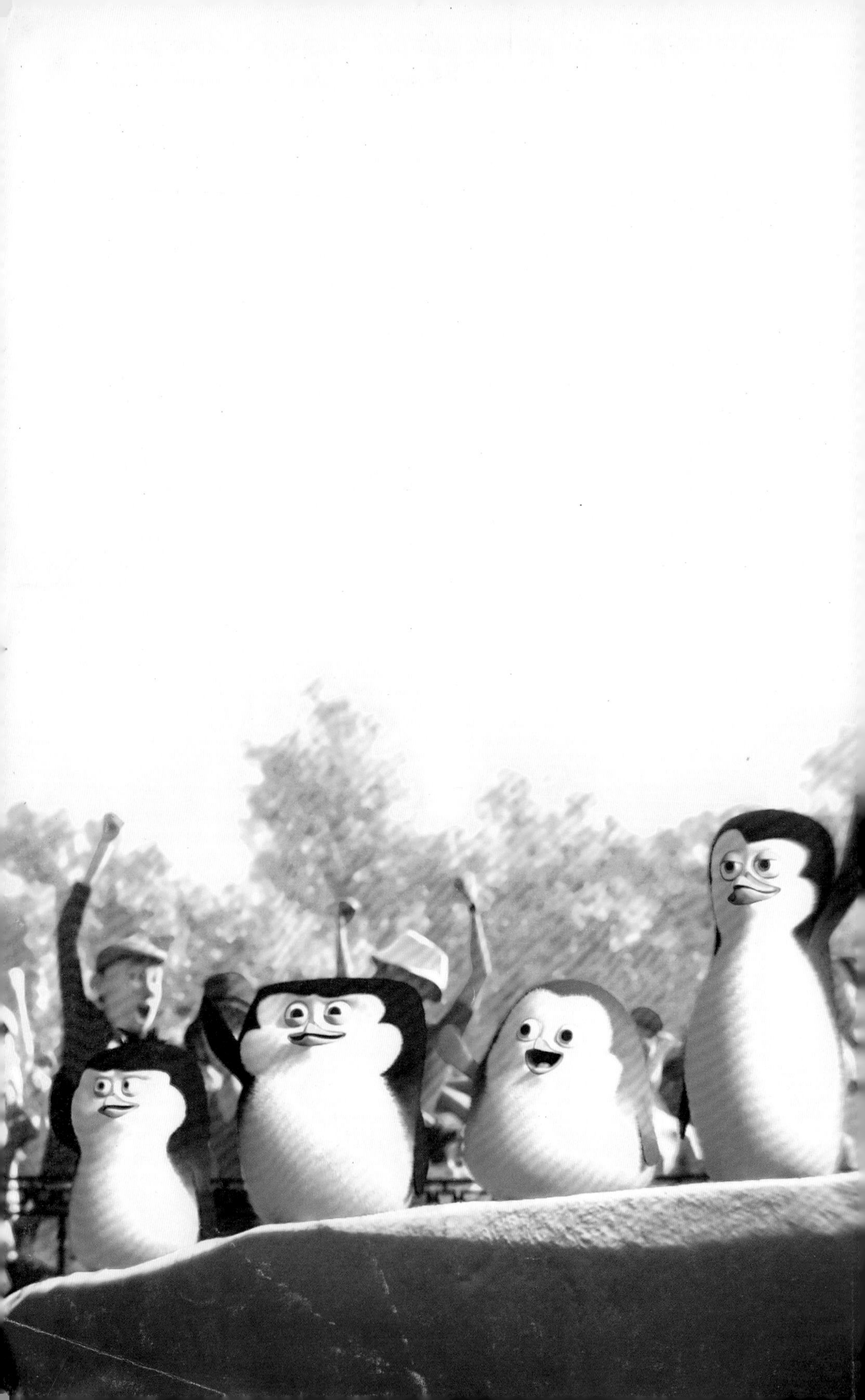